Finding Home

Finding Home
Snow Globe Cafe: Book Two
Copyright © 2019 Kelly J. Calton

ISBN-13: 978-1-7331615-1-0

KELLY J. CALTON

Finding Home

SNOW GLOBE CAFE

BOOK TWO

Chapter 1

SUGAR JONES was frantically pulling clothes out of the boxes that had arrived the day before, looking for the scarf she had ordered for her little girl. The weather had changed, and it was going to snow that afternoon. She shivered just thinking about it. This place was a far cry from San Diego.

It still made her nervous to send her little girl away. Over and over she told herself that everything would be alright. There would be no tears, no panic, and no life-altering internal scars that would never fully heal.

It was just preschool after all, right? Violet had gone all last week and she positively loved it. This was different from her experience. When Sugar was four, she clutched her mother in a vise grip, not wanting to leave her. Kids suffering from ADHD were often immature for their age, and the undiagnosed Sugar was no different. She had been kicked out within a month for bad behavior.

Four-year-old Violet seemed like she couldn't get away from her mom fast enough. "Hurry, Mommy, I'm going to be late!" she said as she looked out the large front window of their apartment. They now lived above a bakery in the small town of Snow Valley, population 2,000. Founded by people of Norwegian descent, the town reminded Sugar of something from a Swiss storybook.

"You are not going to be late," Sugar promised. She produced her cell phone from the back pocket of her jeans. "See, the alarm hasn't gone off yet." The small, open concept apartment looked like a tornado hit it, but she finally produced the scarf. Her daughter's curly blonde hair was in two adorable pigtails, her ice blue eyes looking doubtful at her mother.

They'd only lived here for a couple of weeks. Sugar's mother, Becca, had grown up here but left after her beloved father died to escape an abusive, narcissistic mother. After a huge fight at the funeral, Becca had run to the one place she felt safe, a tree house she shared with the boy she had loved since she was eight years old. Eric Larsson had come to check on her, and after an emotional reunion, they had made love.

Becca left the next day, vowing never to return. She didn't know at the time that she had a stowaway she would later name Sugar. Eric was in a forced, loveless marriage. His father was a violent, cruel man who would do whatever it took to get what he wanted. Fearing for Becca, Eric had gone along with the marriage, and Becca never told Eric about Sugar out of the same fear. John Larsson would do anything to protect his family legacy, and if the rumors were true, even kill for it.

Although it seemed impossible, it was only a couple of weeks since Becca had returned to Snow Valley to claim her inheritance. She couldn't have cared less about the money. Becca was a successful children's author who had created the cultural phenomenon *Beatrice the Butterfly*.

With books, cartoons, merchandising, and movies, Becca would never have to worry about money.

Becca simply wanted two things—her scrapbook with pictures of her father, and his old, worn, leather-bound cookbook that had been passed down in their family for generations. It was a book she knew her daughter would cherish, as she had followed in her grandfather's footsteps and become a baker. Becca had been ecstatic when she found the recipes.

She was less ecstatic when she realized Sugar had followed her to Snow Valley, finding her easily with a tracking app Becca had made her install when she was a teenager. Sugar knew the bare minimum about her mother's life before her, including practically nothing about her father. Once she was old enough, Becca had told her a little about her father, but Sugar didn't buy it. Didn't all women in relationships with married men think that they really didn't love their wives? Becca was very kindhearted, and it pissed Sugar off to no end thinking her father must have taken advantage of her during a very emotional time.

It turns out her mom was right, and her father was in a sham of a marriage. His now ex-wife had confessed she was a lesbian when she was six months pregnant with their twins. Sugar found she had twin siblings who were a little over a year older than her. Alec seemed like a good dude, but Madison was another story altogether.

As she was dressing Violet in her coat and boots, Sugar heard a knock on the door that led to the bakery downstairs. "Grandpa's here!" Violet said as she tore away from Sugar to answer the door.

Becca was busy working on her new children's book,

so only Eric was picking up Violet today. It was always easier when her mom was around, and Sugar had her own suspicions about whether her mother truly needed to finish some work this morning.

Sugar stood up and waited for her father to enter. Her father. It was such a weird concept. She had spent a good portion of her life hating this man she had never met, and now everything was supposed to be sunshine and rainbows. Sugar wasn't a sunshine and rainbows type of woman, and she would need to come to terms with this in her own time.

She had to admit he had been there for her all last week. Her mother had to go back to San Diego for a meeting with her publisher, and Eric stayed behind in case Sugar needed help. It had been hard for her to accept that help, but considering she only had a few days before the newly redesigned Snow Globe Café was set to open, she needed all the help she could get.

Violet's first day of preschool had been terrifying for Sugar. Eric had shown up with his camera and documented the whole experience for Becca. He was quite the presence. Reaching six-foot-four, he shared his blond hair and ice blue eyes with both Sugar and Violet. With chiseled features and a sculpted physique, Eric was quite a head-turner, at least according to Sugar's best friend Emery.

After being assured that she would be called immediately if there were any problems, Sugar left her only child with strangers for the very first time in her life. It was going to be okay. Violet didn't have the struggles Sugar had, and she took after her father in the personality department. Josh had been outgoing and loved to be social.

Sugar wouldn't exactly call herself an introvert, but

she needed her alone time. A party every once in a while was fine, but she needed time to recharge her batteries. Josh had always been the life of the party and couldn't get enough. She pushed down the lump in her throat when she thought about Josh not being here for this or any other milestone in little Violet's life.

Josh had been one of her best friends before they became a couple at fifteen. Along with her other best friend, Emery, he was also her business partner. They had started Sugar Jones LLC back when they were all fifteen, after Emery filmed Sugar's hands making a cupcake that looked like a unicorn. It went viral and they began building the massive web presence that was sugarjones. com. Josh had been a wiz when it came to the technical side, Emery was a master at marketing, and Sugar was the creative force, providing the content.

Why did you have to be such an idiot, Josh? Sugar thought for the umpteenth time. He should have been there for Violet's first day of preschool, but he wasn't. He had died in a fiery car crash when Sugar was five months pregnant. Emery was the only one who knew what had happened the months leading up to the horrifying incident, and Sugar knew she would take what happened the night of the accident to the grave.

They never talked about it, but lately Emery had been bringing Josh up more and more. That always happened around the anniversary of his death at the beginning of October, but it was now November and she still wanted to talk about it more than usual. There wasn't anything they could do about all those things that happened, so why dwell on it? They needed to just keep pushing forward, always moving forward.

"Hi, Sugar," Eric said as he walked into the French country living room, carrying a very excited Violet. Sugar loved this room. It was simple, basic, and beautiful. With a big fireplace that had a polished white mantel and the big storybook windows, it was just Sugar's style.

"Hi," Sugar said, refraining from saying his name. She just couldn't bring herself to call him Dad yet, as the word seemed so foreign on her tongue. Sugar didn't have a cruel bone in her body and could see it bothered him when she called him Eric, so she didn't call him anything at all.

"Thank you again for this," she said. She had a video conference with her Sugar Jones team this morning, and right after that she needed to continue training her new staff downstairs.

It was an impulsive decision for her to stay here and take over the Snow Globe Café with her Sugar Jones brand. Sugar's parents were still very much in love, even after twenty-six years apart, and fell right back in step once reunited. Becca never imagined that Eric could possibly be divorced. She hadn't known that when Eric's dad had died ten years prior, he had immediately ended his marriage.

Becca had hidden well, fearing her mother would find her. She changed her last name from Johansson to Jones and used her middle name Marie as her pen name. Eric looked for her, but when it proved too difficult, he decided that Becca must have remarried and didn't want to upset her life again.

"You don't have to thank me; it's my pleasure," Eric said sincerely. "Downstairs looks amazing. I bet they'll be done with the dining room early."

Sugar's alarm on her phone sprang to life. "Come on, Grandpa, we got to go!" Violet said excitedly. She ran over to her mom as Sugar squatted down to hug her.

"Remember, Grandpa and Grandma are picking you up too, so you can go ice skating," Sugar said, wrapping the bright pink scarf around Violet's neck and putting on her matching hat. "You be a good girl and listen." She put both hands on the sides of her daughter's face. "If you need me, tell Miss Norma to call me, okay?"

Violet rolled her pretty blue eyes. "Okkaaay. I love you, Mommy," she said, hugging her mom once more.

"Love you too, monkey, be good," Sugar said, giving her daughter a loud, smacking kiss. "Thanks again." She held her hand up when Eric started to protest. "I really do appreciate it. You've totally saved me today," she said sincerely.

He kissed Sugar's forehead. He always did this. It was strange, but she was getting used to it. "Like I said, it's no big deal and I should be thanking you for giving me this little girl," he said, fondly smiling at Violet.

Sugar went to the window and watched the two walk down the sidewalk that ran the length of the square. Well, she watched Eric walk as Violet rode tall on his shoulders. She loved being taller than everyone, and she waved at people as they walked down the street toward the preschool.

It really did look like a Swiss storybook. There was a big town square, the kind you find in Europe that's wide open with shiny brick buildings surrounding it. They all had big, happy storybook windows and sloping eaves in bright colors.

It was decked out for the fall season right now, with

pumpkins and a big cornucopia perfect for selfies. All the lights had orange bulbs, giving the square a warm glow at night. She knew they were all getting ready to decorate for Christmas, and she imagined they went all out. This small, charming town was insane when it came to holidays, as drawing tourists to the town was the main source of income for the people who lived there.

A big ice rink was already erected in the square, and Violet had instantly loved it. Sugar had always been incredibly active and that hadn't changed when she had Violet. She just took her along for the ride now. Surfing, climbing, skiing, and most other activities were no stranger to her daughter.

She wondered what all those people thought about Eric walking with his newfound granddaughter. Even though he said it wasn't a big deal, Sugar knew it was. Eric ran and owned a luxury resort simply called The Lodge and was the main employer for most people that lived in this town. The fact that he left work to take his granddaughter to school was a big deal.

Once they were out of sight, Sugar turned to look at the mess she'd made. She always did this and was about to start picking up, when her mind went to a time when she was a little girl.

"How many more days, Mommy?" little Sugar asked as she walked home from kindergarten with her mom.

"Three days and it's summer vacation," Becca said happily. They had almost made it through the year.

"Oh, okay," Sugar said, not able to hide the disappointment in her voice.

Becca stopped and squatted down to her daughter's level, placing her hands on her shoulders. "Did something happen today, sweetheart?" she asked softly. Her little girl felt things so deeply, so much more deeply than other children it seemed.

"Jane had a party for all the kids with birthdays in the summer," Sugar said, her bottom lip quivering a little. "They were all talking about how much fun it was, but I didn't get invited."

Becca hugged her little girl and held her close. Her heart broke in two for her. She knew Sugar could be difficult, but it was cruel to have a party for the whole class and not invite one child. "I'm sure your invitation got lost," Becca said, full well knowing that wasn't true.

"It didn't get lost," Sugar said, pulling away from her mother. "I'm bad. I try not to be, Mommy, I try so hard!" she said, big fat tears falling from her eyes.

Taking her by her shoulders once more, Becca looked directly into Sugar's big blue eyes. "You are not bad, you hear me? How about we play hooky the rest of the week and go climbing?" she asked. There were only a few days left, how much would she miss? Sugar hadn't missed school all year, and even though it didn't seem like the most responsible thing to do, Becca had had it with her little girl being hurt.

"Really?" Sugar asked, her tears drying up and excitement shining from her eyes.

"Really!" Becca said with a laugh, hugging her daughter. She would take her climbing at the rock wall tomorrow, and then after that she was going to find someone who could help her daughter if it meant going to every single doctor in LA.

Sugar was jolted from her train of thought as her phone alarm went off again. It was time for her video conference. She pushed her unshed tears deep down inside. Some wounds never healed. She was still incredibly sensitive but had learned over the years to hide it well because people had exploited her sensitive nature far too many times during her twenty-five years.

⊗

"The creepers are coming out," Vanessa, the admin for Sugar Jones LLC said. "You're already starting to get a lot of emails and calls about the show."

The Sugar Jones brand didn't have a face attached to it for the majority of it's almost ten year existence.

Sugar looked at Vanessa on the computer screen, which also had Emery and Mike, their IT guy. Along with Vanessa and Mike, Sugar Jones LLC employed twenty others, but today's meeting was about the show and how to make the most of the publicity.

"I don't have time to deal with anything from the show," Sugar said. "The bakery is reopening in a few days, and Thanksgiving is next week. I don't want to answer anything about the show until after Christmas."

Emery narrowed her hazel eyes but said nothing.

"I mean it, Em," Sugar said. "I need the time."

"Okay, okay. We won't make any decisions about offers from the show until after Christmas. Are we good for selling cookies, Mike?" Emery asked.

"Totally," Mike said. "I've updated our servers to make sure they can handle the new traffic. Unless forty more million people hit us at once, we're golden."

Emery went on to talk about marketing strategies and aligning when things would be posted on their social media. Sugar completely zoned out, thinking about the bakery. Emery insisted on updating all their servers, including the app they used to sell cookies. Sugar just hoped their online presence would bring people to a real-life bakery.

With everything set and going well with Sugar Jones LLC, she headed down the spiral staircase that led to the bakery to continue training her new staff. Sugar's grandpa had been an epic baker and a beloved member of the community. Sugar knew the minute she walked in this place it was meant to be hers. It was everything she had ever dreamed of, and considering it was already a fully functioning successful bakery, she just needed to put her personal touches here and there to make it her own.

Certainly it was far cry from her home in San Diego, but starting a brand-new business would take so much time away from Violet, even if she would be going to school full-time next year. It would also be terrifyingly risky. Sure, Sugar was successful and had saved to start her dream. Usually risk was something she lived for, but since Violet came along, that instinct to take risks had been curbed by her maternal instinct to be sure her child had a secure future.

For most people, taking on something like this would be daunting at the very least, but not for Sugar. One of the benefits of her condition was hyper focus, and she had focused on this dream most of her life. She had it planned down to the smallest detail in her brain, and if any challenge appeared, her mind simply recalculated how to overcome it, like a navigation system when you make a wrong turn.

Sugar hadn't needed to take those little pills since she was a pre-teen, being one of the fortunate children that seemed to outgrow ADHD. She knew that you never outgrow it; the symptoms are always there, but they just aren't so severe that you need pharmaceutical help. As Becca had always reminded her, there were many good aspects to her differences from other people. Sugar was wildly creative, and her hyper focus truly was a force to be reckoned with when properly channeled.

She still had challenges. Sugar still fought the urge not to interrupt people while they were talking because some exciting thought had jumped into her head. The difference was, she could realize that now, but when she was younger, she just couldn't control it. Sometimes it felt so exhausting, which was why she needed time to recharge after being around large groups of people. So much stimuli just wore her down.

After she had run the new staff through their paces, she left them to practice the new desserts that would go on the menu. She had worried how these people would react to a twenty-five-year-old taking charge, but her worries were in vain. They had realized right off the bat that she knew what she was doing.

She did know what she was doing. Sugar had been baking since she could stand on a chair and whisk. Her mother, grieving her father, had made his recipes over and over. It was also the only thing that seemed to hold little Sugar's attention, so Becca had done everything she could to foster that talent. Sugar had graduated from culinary school at the top of her class by eighteen, interned for a year in Paris, and worked in various bakeries since she was twelve.

All this was accomplished on top of being the creative head of a popular online presence, one that would come in handy when promoting the newly branded café. She could literally reach millions without spending a dime once they opened in a week. In the past, people had shown up in droves when Sugar did an event, but she was still nervous. They were over an hour from the nearest big city. A part of her worried that people wouldn't come out.

The television show would help also. Set to come out the weekend before Thanksgiving, Sugar had participated in a popular holiday baking show that was on network television every year. At five-foot-ten with curves in all the right places, Sugar knew why they wanted her on the show. She was to be the blonde Barbie doll that would provide comic relief for a week or two until she was voted off.

They didn't know how wrong they were. It was a constant battle while shooting. The producers tried to talk her into wearing high heels and ridiculous dresses. She had refused, sticking to her ever present yoga pants and kitchen appropriate mules. She couldn't do anything about the hair and makeup people though, and she knew the elaborate updos and how they accentuated her big blue eyes and full lips was out of her hands.

She was the only internet personality in the competition, so she had a lot to prove. Sure, her confections looked beautiful, but now was her chance to prove she had actual chops. Exceeding that expectation, Sugar had walked away with the competition full of professional pastry chefs. How she would translate on television was anyone's guess since they piece together different phrases in reality TV, creating the character they want, but as Emery said, any publicity is good publicity.

Sugar doubted they would want the winner to look bad, so she wasn't worried. Signing an NDA, she wasn't allowed to tell anyone that she won, and that was the hardest part now. Sure, her good mood had said it all after that last day of shooting, but it had been overshadowed by the whole Becca going home situation. Now that that had been settled, it would be very hard for Sugar to keep her mouth shut.

"Mr. Hanson, it looks amazing in here!" Sugar said as she entered the main dining room. Eric was right, this man was at least three days ahead of schedule. She was sure it didn't hurt that her newly discovered father and main employer for the town had stood in the background with a watchful eye while Sugar laid out what she needed done to the café. Normally something like that would piss Sugar off, but since she was on a tight schedule, she begrudgingly kept her mouth shut.

Mr. Hanson, a kindly older gentleman, wiped his brow with a big handkerchief. "Thank you," he said. "We might be finished by the end of the day tomorrow." Sugar had been pleasantly surprised that they could unseal the kitchen area that morning.

"I can't tell you how much I appreciate this," Sugar said sincerely, smiling her charming smile that produced one tiny dimple above her left lip.

The wood floors had been stripped and polished, the walls painted a comfortable butter yellow, and they were finishing up installing the new espresso machines. A storage room had been opened to give more room in the dining area, and once the new tables and bakery case were installed, she'd be set.

"It was my pleasure," he said with a slight blush on his cheeks. "We can come back and install your photos once the paint has cured a few more days," he said, pointing to the large photo prints that were lying on one of their work tables.

"Good, good," Sugar said distractedly as she ran her hand over the large picture of her grandfather and Becca. She wished she could have known him.

Hans Johansson seemed like such a good man stuck in a horrible situation. He had married Becca's mom, Greta, late in life and realized how mentally ill she was too late. Hans protected Becca as much as he could from Greta's narcissism, but in a time where fathers seldom got custody of their children, he had been afraid to leave her.

"The Andersons should be here any minute with the tables," Mr. Hanson said.

Jackson Anderson. He was another story altogether. A tall, twenty-seven-year-old drink of water with romance-novel long, dirty blond hair, aqua blue eyes, and a wicked smile, he demanded attention. Loaded with muscles that came from actual work, he was a man's man.

She couldn't deny she was attracted to him. Most women would be, but for Sugar it was more than that and she didn't like it one bit. A distraction was not something she could afford right now, and that's all he could be. Sugar wasn't good with relationships. She learned that much during her years with Josh.

Add to that fact that he was also a part of the three families that owned The Lodge, even a casual hookup with him was impossible. Three families had come together back around World War II to build what would become a thriving business for the rich and famous. Jackson's family, the Andersons, were the builders. The

Olssons were old money with connections, and her family, the Larssons, ran it all. Together the three families brought a specific skill set that made it a wild success.

There was a knock at the front door, and Sugar looked up to see Jackson standing there. He gave her one of his heartbreaker smiles as she went to unlock the door.

"Hey," Sugar said as she leaned on the door.

"Hey yourself," Jackson said. "We've got your tables."

Paul Anderson, Jackson's father, made custom furniture now that he was retired. He jumped right in when Sugar said she wanted something different, and she couldn't wait to see them.

She started to go outside, and he stopped her. "It's cold and about to start snowing. We'll bring them in." This might be the first time she saw him with an actual coat on, and his long wavy blonde hair tucked under a black knit hat. It accentuated his aqua blue eyes, and his fit-just-right jeans accentuated something else as Sugar watched him get the first table out of the truck and bring it inside.

Sugar could barely contain her excitement. The tables were exactly what she wanted. "Jackson, your dad is the best! I can't believe how perfect these are!"

Jackson smiled as Sugar ran her hand down the white-washed pine table. "Yes, he is. I hope you like the chairs just as much."

Her hands flew to her mouth when he brought them in. She had found the colorful mosaic tiles while on vacation with Emery right before she became pregnant with Violet. She had immediately fallen in love with them and knew one day she would incorporate them into her bakery. Everything else was simple and clean, but the mosaic inlays with different shades of blue, yellow, and pink added just the right amount of happy.

The chairs were the same bleached wood as the tables, and the backs had a cutout to perfectly fit the tiles. Sugar squatted down to admire the craftsmanship, and Jackson joined her.

"They are perfect. The way the tile sits in the back, well, I couldn't have asked for anything more," Sugar said as she gave Jackson a big smile.

"Thanks," he said as he ran his hand down the side of the mosaic. "This was a bitch to cut out."

"You made the chairs?" Sugar asked, tilting her head to the side.

Jackson chuckled. "My dad likes to keep busy, but tile is not his thing."

It really was nice how it seemed everyone was coming together to help her. Foreign, but nice. Growing up it was always her mom and her against the world, and she had to admit it was lovely having others around.

"Well, they are perfect. Thank you," she said, giving him that smile again.

He really was a great guy. Although she hadn't spent a lot of time with him, he was always nice and funny, and Violet instantly loved him. He had driven them home after the big Halloween ball a couple of weeks ago, and the two of them had a wonderful conversation.

How many single guys in their late twenties leave a big party to help get a tired little girl home? In Sugar's eyes he was a good dude, and if she was interested in something more, he'd be first on her list. She definitely couldn't deny the attraction, and even with her limited experience, she was pretty sure it was mutual.

"Thanks. I had a few mosaics left over, but there was a little project I wanted to do," Jackson said. "I can't tell you what because it's a surprise."

The men that came with Jackson were now bringing in the rest of the chairs, and Sugar started arranging them around the tables. "I hate surprises," she said, "but if you do work this good, I'm willing to risk it."

"You won't regret it," he said as he helped her arrange the chairs.

"Doesn't working at the hotel keep you busy enough?" Sugar asked.

Jackson crossed his arms on the top of one of the chairs and leaned on it. "I like taking planks of wood or tile or metal and making something useful. To me that isn't work." Jackson shrugged. "It's like my entertainment."

Sugar pulled out one of the chairs and sat down, testing it out. They were comfortable too.

"I know what you mean. I'd stay home and bake a cake before going to a big party any day."

Sugar jumped up out of the chair. "Speaking of which, hold on one second."

She disappeared into the kitchen and came back with a big box of treats her new employees were making to practice for the big day.

"We may need to make some more tables if this is the tip," Jackson said. "Thank you."

"No problem," Sugar said as she handed him the large box. "Make sure you give some to your dad," she warned.

"Not making any promises," Jackson smiled as he and the workers headed out.

She watched him pull away and went back into the kitchen. Her whole being buzzed with excitement as she saw the bakers busily working on her recipes. She'd asked the current employees if they knew of anyone with some knowledge of culinary arts who'd be interested in a job. She had lucked out once again that there were plenty of people to choose from.

"I think it's going well," Jacob said. He had been an employee prior to Sugar's arrival and had been trained by the last baker that had worked with her grandfather. Jacob was good, dependable, and excited for the chance to run the night shift. The promotion would be a blessing to him, but more than that, his kids wouldn't have to get up at the crack of dawn to go to childcare before school anymore.

Like many of the people that lived in Snow Valley, his wife commuted for work, which was fine during the summer, but the winters could be treacherous. There was a train that went to the closest big city, but that took longer than driving. She could easily have a twelve-hour day in the winter between the travel and work.

"It really is," Sugar said, picking up a sugar cookie and breaking it in half to examine the crumb. These would be the bread and butter of the bakery. They would sell some there, but most would be sold online with the Sugar Jones Cookie Alert app. Decorated cookies took time, but they were profitable and sold out in seconds when people would get the alert that some were available for sale.

Janet, the general manager who kept this place running after her grandfather passed, had been skeptical about all the new employees, but Sugar knew these cookies would pay all the bills and salaries for the month. Sure, it would be a much higher volume than Sugar Jones had ever put out before, but Emery was convinced they could sustain the volume indefinitely.

She tasted the cookie as the bakers stood there nervously watching. Sugar was a perfectionist and didn't hold back on her critiques. These cookies needed to be perfect, and unless she was honest, they wouldn't get there. A big smile broke across her face. "I think you got it," she said as the bakers clapped and shouted gleefully.

The cookie alert was the last thing Josh had made for the Sugar Jones app. Even though his intentions for it still pissed Sugar off, she was grateful for it now. It had helped keep her sane when she needed to bake for actual people, even if she didn't get to see them enjoying her efforts.

"If I ever stop throwing up, I'm going to kill you," Sugar said as she left the small bathroom for the third time that day. She found Josh sitting at his little work desk in their small apartment, pounding away on the keyboard as always.

"What?" he asked, looking up. His face softened when he saw his ashen looking wife. "I'm sorry, babe, I really wanted to get this finished. You okay?"

She plopped down on their secondhand brown loveseat. "Yes, I'm just really sick of puking. When did the book say it stops?"

Josh picked up his laptop and went to sit by Sugar. "Soon, I promise," he said, putting his arm around her. "I have something I hope will make you feel better." He opened the app on the computer, and a wild screen that shouted COOKIE ALERT! in bright pink colors came to life.

Sugar looked at the screen curiously. "What's that?"

"That," he said, pointing to the flashing screen, "is how you can sell cookies online. You can do it at your own pace, and when you have some available, the cookie alert will pop up on people's app. I bet there will be a big demand, and since people will

never know when you'll have them available, they'll snap them up quick."

"That's genius," Sugar said with a huge smile. She had been working for a local bakery and loved it, but once the baby came it would get difficult. The plans she had to start her own bakery were already pushed back by years since her surprise pregnancy, so this was something that could keep her own creative juices flowing.

He moved in for a kiss and Sugar backed away. Seeing that hurt look he got on his face sometimes, she pointed to her cheek. "I just threw up everything I ate and probably everything you ate too. I don't think you want to kiss me right now," she teased.

"Unlike you, I always want to kiss." His demeanor had totally changed, but Sugar refused to take the bait. His insecurities made her feel like she was in a closed off room that was slowly being sucked of air, and even though she was pregnant with his child and married to him, it didn't seem to make a damn bit of difference.

Sugar took his hand and held it to her lips. "Thank you, Josh, thank you so much. I love it."

Placated, he relaxed. "You're welcome." He shut the laptop and kissed her on the cheek. "I was thinking that with this option in play, maybe we should just buy a house."

"We aren't ready for that, Josh," Sugar protested. True, they made good money with the Sugar Jones brand and Josh's side work as a programmer, but they needed to save for the bakery and the future. It would be another fight for sure, as Josh's version of the perfect house would be big, and Sugar preferred small and functional.

"But now that we have this app, do you really need to start a bakery?" he asked. "You could quit your job now too, especially with how bad you've been feeling."

Sugar pulled back. "I love my job. It's not about the money, Josh, and you know it. I need to work, and owning a bakery in the future is my dream." She got a pit in her stomach when she realized he didn't create the app to make her feel better; he made it to keep her home. She could feel more air being sucked out of the room.

He got up and went back to his desk without a word. This had been a continual fight since Sugar had become pregnant and they got married. Deep down, he knew he was being unreasonable. These were all things he knew about Sugar and they had been planning for it since they had both graduated. He knew her dream was to open a bakery. That hadn't changed once she found out they would be parents, and probably nothing would change it.

He should just be grateful that Sugar had forgiven him after Emery told Sugar his secret, but he couldn't help wishing that for once he could be number one in Sugar's life. "I just don't want our child to grow up like I did, in a little cracker box."

Sugar got up and went and sat on his lap. "I like our little cracker box." She laid her head on his shoulder. "It's not forever, you know, just until we're more secure."

"I know," he said and put his arms around her, holding her close.

Josh was brilliant and made the decision to make a full on app for Sugar Jones LLC to go with the website and social media accounts. He didn't want the company to ever be dependent on other companies like Facebook and Twitter. Many an influencer lost when snapchat died, but that would never happen to Sugar. Josh made sure they were in firm control of their own destinies.

"Look at those feet!" One of Sugar's new employees shook her back to Earth, proud of the French macaroons that had just come out of the oven. Sugar smiled. The red velvet macaroons were shiny with perfect domes. Yes, things were coming together nicely.

Sugar's watch vibrated. The text from Eric said he had picked up Violet and was on his way to the ice rink. Violet had fallen in love with skating when Sugar took her the other day, and she was glad she was getting to enjoy it again this afternoon. Violet took after Sugar when it came to athletics. She was a natural.

The buzzer to the back door rang out, and Sugar looked up into the newly installed security monitor. The afternoon delivery was here. She had been waiting for this all day. Sugar had ordered shipping boxes with the new branding, and she had been anxious to see how they turned out.

Eric had insisted on installing The Lodge's state-of-the-art security system in both the bakery and the apartment. Sugar had tried to protest, but considering her mother technically still owned it all, she was outvoted. Deep down, she knew he was right. She was about to be on national television, and they needed to make sure Violet was safe. She also learned that although he seemed laid back and accommodating, Eric Larsson was a man who got what he wanted.

"It's about to really start coming down," the young deliveryman said when Sugar opened the door. He started unloading the boxes she had ordered for the cookies. She opened one and inspected it. "Snow Globe Café with Sugar Jones" was emblazoned across the top. They were perfect.

"Violet is going to be so thrilled," Sugar sighed. Her daughter had been so excited when she heard it was supposed to snow today. Becca and Sugar had taken Violet skiing last year, but she insisted she didn't remember what snow was like.

"Why don't you take them some of these cookies?" Jacob said. "I got this."

Sugar grabbed her skates and made it to the rink just as the snowflakes started to fall. It was just across the street from the café, and she found them easily with Eric's tall physique standing out in the small crowd.

"Grandpa, Grandpa, it's snowing!" Violet shouted excitedly as Eric picked her up and spun her around, laughing with delight. Becca looked on adoringly at two of her favorite people.

Sugar's cell vibrated and she saw a perfectly timed picture. Her half-brother Alec was standing on the other side of the rink, and snapped the picture just in time with his cell phone. With big, fat snowflakes falling all around them, they looked like they belonged on an old-fashioned Christmas card.

Eric was holding Violet high in the air, his long black coat swirling as she threw her arms wide open and tilted her head up to the sky, trying to catch snowflakes with her tongue. Becca stood in the background with a big smile on her face and a loving look in her eyes.

She quickly texted the picture to Becca and Emery, remembering to add Eric to the group text at the last minute. Eric and Becca noticed Sugar sitting on a bench putting her skates on at the edge of the rink and skated over.

"Taking a break?" Eric asked.

"Just for a minute," Sugar said as Violet scrambled out of Eric's arms.

"Mommy!" Violet haphazardly skated to her mother

as Sugar laughed and held her arms wide open to catch her. Oh, how she had missed this kid today. Until the television show started shooting, she hadn't been away from her for more than a few hours at a time. It was still hard for Sugar to leave her, but she knew Violet needed time with other people too.

"How was school?" Sugar enveloped her in a big bear hug. Violet looked so happy. When she was her age, school started and ended in tears. Even though Violet had been going to school for a week, the relief still flooded her knowing her child wouldn't have the same struggles she had.

"We made snowflakes and sang songs, and Mommy, we got a turtle!" Violet had been begging for a pet. She loved animals, but with their small apartment back in San Diego, it just wasn't feasible. Sugar would seriously consider it if they decided to stay in the area after the holidays, but for now that needed to be on the back burner.

Sugar passed her cell to her mom.

"Oh Alec, this picture is wonderful," Becca said as she gave Alec a charming smile.

"No big deal," Alec said. "Hey California, you going to be alright on those skates?" he teased.

"Pppsssh, whatever," Sugar said as she stood up and zoomed past him. She may have been raised in Southern California, but Becca took her ice skating at the local hockey rink all the time.

Before she knew it, they were racing each other with Violet cheering them from the side. Eric was laughing and Becca was just shaking her head.

The loud whistle from the rink guard killed their fun just as Sugar was about to win.

"Larsson, you know better than that," the burly rink guard warned.

Chastised, they skated to the side of the rink, both smiling once out of eyesight of the guard. Having a brother might not be all that bad.

Chapter 2

JACKSON ANDERSON sanded the side of the pint-sized table with a skilled hand. He needed to make sure it was completely smooth, as he didn't want little Violet getting any splinters. The smell of sawdust and wood filled his father's workshop where craftsmen were working double-time to finish the new tables for the Snow Globe Café.

He liked the new concept. Long community tables in a simple white pine would replace most of the old ones, with a sprinkling of more intimate tables for people that wanted privacy. The chairs had colorful mosaic inlays that Sugar had bought over five years ago. She wasn't kidding when she said she had been planning for years. The mixture of the simple and the complex was perfection.

From what he knew of Sugar so far, that seemed to describe her also. She was gorgeous but did absolutely nothing to play it up. Reaching at least five-foot-ten with long, wavy blonde hair that nearly reached her waist, and a slim figure with just the right amount of curves, she could have been a model instead of a baker.

The few times he saw her this week she didn't have a stitch of makeup on and had her long blonde hair braided or in a topknot on her head. She seemed to be fond of yoga pants, and half the time he saw her, she didn't even match, like getting dressed was an after-thought. He had never met a woman like this, and it fascinated him. Of course, it didn't hurt that she didn't need the makeup and would have looked like perfection in a potato sack.

His mind wandered way too many times when he was alone in the last week to the Halloween ball. It was tradi-tion that all the families from The Lodge take a picture, and Eric had insisted that the newly found Sugar and her daughter be in the picture. Sugar had dressed as Wonder Woman, and just the thought of her in that costume sent him into a lust-filled tizzy.

He didn't even want to think about those ice blue eyes that seemed to see right through to his soul, or that full mouth. No, he didn't need to think about that dimple that showed above her lip when she smiled a big genuine smile, or how it had become his goal to get at least one dimple every time he saw her.

He pulled out the small drawer he made to hold Violet's art supplies, testing it to make sure it was easy to open and close. His father Paul had taken on making the new tables, and when they had visited the café to talk with her, Jackson noticed Violet drawing away on an old card table, sitting on her knees to get a better vantage point.

No, Jackson didn't want to think about how it had touched his heart when a few days later Violet gave him a present—a picture with a little girl with blonde pigtails holding hands with a giant man with long hair. He had only put it on his refrigerator because he didn't want to hurt the little girl's feelings. He ignored the little voice that told him chances of her seeing it there were slim to none.

"I don't remember that being part of the project." His father had entered the shop, and Jackson couldn't help but notice how all the carpenters seemed to stand just a little bit straighter, work just a little bit harder.

"Oh, um, I felt bad for the kid drawing on that rickety table, so I used some of the scraps from the project to make her something sturdier," Jackson explained as he worked intently.

Paul tried to hide his knowing smile and said nothing. Jackson appreciated it.

Paul said as he squatted down to inspect the table. It had been made with great care. "This is really good work, son," he said. "Are you going to use the leftover mosaics for the little chairs?"

"Thanks." Jackson ran his hand along the top, checking to make sure it was perfectly smooth. "That's the plan, so they match the dining room chairs." Paul had taught him everything he knew, and Jackson couldn't have loved or respected him more if he tried.

He looked up to him, and when people compared him to his father, it was the best compliment he could receive. Paul never got caught up in the money or luxury bullshit from The Lodge. He was his own man, and now that he had handed most of his duties to Jackson, he kept himself busy making furniture. Jackson imagined the day that he stopped being busy would be the day he died, and he couldn't bear to think about that.

It was the whole reason he had decided to stay in Snow Valley. Paul had always encouraged him to get out and see the rest of the world and not let Snow Valley be his entire life. Along with Eric's son, Alec, he had spent many summers with his maternal grandparents in Alabama, seeing what life was like when you weren't the crowned prince of a small town. They were farmers and expected both boys to pull their weight, and they learned about the rewards a good work ethic could produce.

When he graduated high school at seventeen, he had joined the army, and he saw too much of the world. The simple life of Snow Valley seemed like heaven after some of his experiences, and when his father had a health scare, that cinched it. Jackson's parents had met later in life, and his dad was ten years older than his mother.

After a wildfire destroyed some of the property they owned away from The Lodge, his father had stood with Jackson and Alec when they proposed building a new hotel—a smaller boutique hotel with less emphasis on luxury and more on the experience. People stayed at the Snow Valley Hotel because they wanted to experience the town and all the activities that came with mountain living, not to be pampered.

They also had forty hook-ups for people with mobile tiny homes and RV's. He knew he didn't have the luxury of time with his dad like someone else who was twenty-seven. His dad was in his early seventies, so Jackson didn't want to waste a minute away from him.

He shouldn't waste time feeling sorry for himself. There were others that had it much worse. Poor little Violet didn't have a father and Sugar had to raise her all alone. Cursing himself, he pulled a notebook from his back pocket to start a rough sketch of the chairs as his dad went to get the left-over mosaics. It seemed his mind wandered to those two constantly and he needed to stop it.

Jackson had his life all planned out. He would live it up like his father had until he was at least thirty-five and then he would settle down and have a family. He loved kids. His parents had wanted more, but his mother had an emergency hysterectomy a year after he was born.

Jackson would have enough kids to make a basketball team if he could. Lucky for him, he had grown up with Eric's kids, so he never felt the loneliness of being an only child. Alec couldn't be more of a brother to him even if they did share DNA, and Madison was his bratty kid sister, even if she didn't see it that way in the past.

His mind wandered to Sugar once more as he wondered if she wanted more kids. *Dammit*, he thought. She was just something new in town and that's why he was so captivated. Their families were indefinitely tied together, so a casual fling was not a good idea. There was also a child involved, and Jackson didn't get involved with women who had children. Not because he didn't love children, but because he didn't want them to get hurt when he wasn't around anymore.

Jackson thought about grabbing his phone and checking out Tinder. Maybe he just needed a little distraction, and living in an area full of people on vacation, it was never an issue finding someone that wanted to be distracted. He never dated anyone from either of their hotels, following his father's golden rule, but there were plenty others right outside Snow Valley.

He didn't think there was anything wrong with two consenting adults enjoying each other, but the thought quickly left his mind as his father came back with the mosaics. Violet was going to love these chairs.

CR

Sugar bent down and peeked in the oven. Dinner was coming along nicely, and her homemade mac and cheese would be done soon. It was Violet's choice, and she had been so very good this last week. Emery and Alec should be there any minute now, and Sugar couldn't wait to see her best friend. Emery and her family were Sugar's adoptive family. Growing up with Becca being the only blood relative she had, both Sugar and Becca were grateful to Emery and her parents.

Emery's mother, Laura, was also the agent that broke *Beatrice the Butterfly*, and her father, Avery, was Becca's lawyer. They spent holidays together, and whenever there was a daddy-daughter dance, Avery Cooper always made sure to take Sugar as well as Emery. They were just good people.

Emery was going to stay in the other apartment above the bakery during the holiday season. Along with Sugar Jones LLC, she also ran an internet marketing company. When Sugar had hunted down her mother last week, Emery had come along for the ride in case Sugar needed her. That was just the kind of friend she was.

Even during the chaos that followed Sugar's presence, Emery had managed to snag not only Alec and Jackson's Snow Valley Hotel as a new client, but the town's chamber of commerce. Money for advertising was scarce for the new Snow Valley Hotel, and Emery had convinced them that with social media, they could get all the attention they needed to keep their hotel booked.

Emery was taking the train in from the airport, and Alec had agreed to pick her up. Emery wasn't keen on driving during the first snowfall of the year, and Sugar didn't drive at all unless it was necessary. Sugar's big SUV had been delivered the other day and it would be available whenever Emery needed it.

The camera at the bottom of the stairs in the alley that led to the apartment picked up movement, and a small pop-up appeared on the large television screen over the fireplace that was currently playing Violet's favorite movie, *Trolls*. Sugar could repeat every single bit of dialog from that damn movie. Hell, sometimes she even dreamt about it. It didn't seem to matter what they tried to get her to watch, she always landed back on wanting to watch that movie.

The screen showed Emery climbing the stairs with a small overnight bag and Alec struggling with two armloads of suitcases. "They're here!" Violet ran to the door excitedly.

"Hold up, monkey, it's cold." Sugar grabbed the spare keys to the other apartment and wrapped the quilt from her chair around her shoulders. Opening the door, she shivered as the cold air hit her. She didn't know if she could ever get used to being cold all the time.

Emery let out a screech and threw her arms around Sugar. "I missed your face," she said, hugging her friend tightly.

"I missed yours too." It was so good to have part of her support system back. Now that both her mom and Emery were here, everything seemed right with the world.

"Auntie Em! Auntie Em!" Violet shouted, standing away from the door. One year Sugar was going to talk

Emery into dressing as an elderly lady and Violet as Dorothy for Halloween if it was the last thing she did.

Emery dropped her bag and scooped Violet up in a great big hug. "Oh, how I missed you, little monkey." Emery smelled the little girl's hair as she hugged her, taking in the scent of the baby shampoo that she missed so much.

"Little help here," Alec called from outside the door. Sugar handed her the keys to the apartment next door and Emery smiled apologetically as she went back outside to the balcony that led to the second apartment.

Sugar smiled a little when she saw them go back down the stairs on the security camera. She knew there was no way that was all Emery had brought to stay a couple of months. A weekend, maybe, but where Sugar picked her clothes for functionality and comfort, Emery was all about the latest styles. She loved fashion.

Emery was the ying to Sugar's yang. They were so different in every way, and it just worked. They were both tall and thin, but that's where the similarities stopped. Emery's father was white, and her mother was African American and Mexican. Stunning in her own right, Emery's mocha skin highlighted her beautiful hazel eyes, bright wide smile, and high cheek bones. Her long curly brunette hair was usually in a tidy ponytail or a neat headband. The two of them together always attracted a lot of attention.

Sugar was fond of saying that Emery was her soulmate, which Emery insisted was the most depressing thing she had ever heard.

Sugar took the mac and cheese out of the oven as Emery and Alec came back in. "I smell a little child," Alec said wickedly while making pinching gestures with his hands. Violet yelped and ran, but he caught up quickly with his long legs. He picked her up and flipped her upside down, giving her a great big raspberry on her tummy as she giggled uncontrollably.

He took to being an uncle like a duck to water. Easygoing and patient, Alec had quickly become one of Violet's favorite people. Sugar couldn't seem to turn around without bumping into him or Eric, and she was starting to get used to it even if it was hard for her to let new people in. It was easier with Alec. You just couldn't help but like him.

Alec looked over the small butcher block island that separated the living room from the kitchen and took a great big sniff. "That smells awesome. What are you guys going to eat?" he asked, winking at Sugar. He notoriously had a huge appetite, and like Sugar, didn't seem to gain an ounce.

"If you can eat this whole pan, I'll make you an apple pie every night for a week," Sugar dared. She had made her famous apple pie for the first family dinner they had, and Alec had been dreaming about it ever since.

"Give me a fork," he said seriously.

"Stop." Emery said. "I've heard what happens when you two start egging each other on." Sugar knew Violet told Emery all about their ice skating race because Emery gave her a long lecture about how it wasn't a good time for broken bones.

"You are no fun," Alec pouted.

"Oh, you have no idea, mister," Emery said, shaking her fork at him. "I've given you several assignments to complete and you haven't finished one of them."

Sugar smiled and patted Alec on the back. "Welcome

to the club. It's best just to do what she says and make no sudden movements. Come on, let's eat."

Sugar and Emery sat in the comfortable living room after dinner as Alec read Violet a bedtime story in her new room. They both smiled as they heard his voice go up a couple of octaves when he read the girl part. Violet has insisted Alec read her story tonight as Sugar tended to not follow the story.

Sugar's mind would start to make up her own story as she read, and now that Violet was learning words, she realized it. It wouldn't be long before Violet figured out that Cinderella had not said screw it all and became a doctor.

"This place looks great." Emery had expected to walk into a complete disaster. Sugar was the messiest person she knew, unless it was the kitchen. She would meticulously clean the kitchen until it shined but would leave her whole wardrobe on the floor. Emery knew it was part of Sugar's lingering ADHD symptoms, but being a neat freak, it drove her nuts.

"Why so surprised?" Emery narrowed her eyes and Sugar laughed. "Okay, fine. I hired a housekeeper. My mom said if I didn't, she'd send one herself." Becca had been terrified that she'd return in a week and have to search for her little granddaughter under piles of papers and clothes.

Normally Sugar hated anything that seemed like a needless indulgence, but knowing her new housekeeper was trying to make ends meet while she finished college, comforted her. She hated to admit it, but it was nice coming back to the apartment after a long day to find all the new clothes she had ordered were put away and everything was tidy.

"Violet wants you." Alec had come back to the living room after he finished the story. Violet may have enjoyed hearing a story read word for word, but nobody tucked her in like Mommy.

After tucking her in and kissing her sweet little cheek, Sugar went back to the living room, leaving Violet's door open a crack. Alec and Emery were arguing.

"I will not do that," Alec protested. "Sugar, did you know your friend is a sexist? She's trying to get me to send her naked pics."

Emery rolled her eyes. "Shirtless is a long way from naked."

Sugar plopped down in the comfortable blue wing-back chair, pulling the quilt around her. "She's in marketing, what did you expect?" Sugar couldn't help but be happy that Emery's relentless drive to succeed was being directed at someone else.

"Look, I don't make the rules," Emery said, taking a sip of her wine.

"So you just exploit them?" Alec asked.

"Exactly!"

Sugar hid her own smile behind her wine glass as Alec opened his mouth to speak but closed it, dumbfounded. This was Sugar's version of a perfect night, just sitting around with a couple of friends, enjoying good conversation, food, and wine. Who needed crowded clubs, parties, and binding clothes?

"You need to trust me, Alec," Emery said. "Have I steered you wrong so far? Besides, Jackson already sent me some of his." Sugar's ears perked up at this. She was going to have to check out their Instagram.

"Fine." Alec crossed his arms across his chest. "But it's

your fault when Jackson's feelings get hurt that people like my pic more than his."

Emery held her wine glass up. "I'll take full responsibility." Men were so easy.

Secretly she wondered which one of them would do better on Insta. Jackson had it going on, no doubt. He was a big dude and his muscles seemed to have muscles. There was an air of danger about him with his long hair and close-trimmed beard.

He also seemed more driven than Alec, and faithfully completed all the assignments Emery had sent him. She got the impression that Alec was just along for the ride.

Even though he was her brother Sugar could acknowledge he was attractive, extremely attractive in his own right, and she had no doubt he had his share of muscles even though his physique wasn't as large as Jackson's. Alec had more of a swimmer's body, and he shared those classic Norwegian good looks with his father. His blond hair was just a little too long, curling around his collar, and his lips were almost to pretty to be on a man.

Yes, it was a crap shoot to see who would do best. Jackson was more a man's man, and Alec was more boy band member all grown up.

After she finished her wine, Emery excused herself for the night. "It's driving her crazy that her suitcases aren't unpacked," Sugar confided to Alec.

He was putting his coat on and getting ready to leave too. "I have suitcases from the Fourth of July that I still haven't unpacked."

Sugar burst out laughing. "Me too."

He surprised her by giving her a great big hug. "Thanks for letting Dad help you this week," he said sincerely. "It's kind of his thing, helping his kids. He doesn't show it, but he's really sensitive. Spending time with you and Violet has meant the world to him."

Sugar swallowed the lump that formed in her throat, pushing it deep down with all the other lumps over the years. "It's not a problem. I don't know what I would have done this week without him," she said honestly. "And you. Thank you so much for all your help. I really do appreciate it."

"Are you kidding? I now have an awesome niece. Someone's got to take care of me when I'm old," he joked. "Add the fact that I have a sister that can almost beat me on the rink, well, no thanks are necessary."

"That's bullshit, I would have beaten you, and you know it!"

"Ha! Then I guess you aren't scared of a rematch. If Josie Stranton is working this week, it's on. She had a crush on me in high school," he explained with a toothy grin.

"Bring it, buddy," Sugar said as she wished her brother a good night. Brother. She could get used to having one of those.

Chapter 3

SUGAR WAS GETTING NERVOUS. Opening day was getting closer and closer. She knew she should listen to Emery. Ever since the network had starting running promos for the show this last weekend, the Sugar Jones app had eighty thousand more downloads on Google Play and iTunes. They had never come close to experiencing a jump like that before.

The ad for *The Holiday Baking Extravaganza* had prominently featured Sugar. Violet counted that Sugar was shown five times. Sugar running across the kitchen, joking with the host, rolling her eyes at a fellow competitor, piping a cookie, and her personal favorite, tilting her head to the side and whispering, "Boom." She just hoped they televised why she had done that. The bastard deserved it.

Yes, she knew she should listen to Emery, but she couldn't help but be nervous. She hired a lot of people, and she felt the weight of being responsible for their employment. Some of them had quit other jobs to work for her, grateful to be working close to home.

If cookie production was any indicator, she had nothing to worry about. The nightshift at the bakery was up and running, and every box placed online sold out in seconds. Janet, her general manager, was amazed by the amount of money coming in. They had always sold out in no time at all, but they had never done this much volume before.

She knew she couldn't charge four or five dollars for a decorated cookie in this small town, but online that was nothing. Sugar paid her employees a good wage for the standard of living here, and the online sales were the only thing that made it possible.

She pulled her coat tighter as the cold wind gusted across the square. Jesus, it was cold here. Sugar was heading to the local floral shop to see if they could make a centerpiece for the big snow globe shaped window at the café. At the Halloween ball she had admired the work they had done, and she needed the window to be perfect.

It would only be there a short time since it would be changed for Christmas the day after Thanksgiving, and Sugar liked the idea of having something living. "Can I have your autograph?" a voice called from behind her.

Sugar turned and rolled her eyes. Emery looked like she had grown up here her whole life with her plaid peacoat, red scarf, and matching beret. "You're funny."

"Jesus, Sugar, what are you wearing?" Emery had ordered most of the new clothes Sugar and Violet needed when they moved to a cold climate, and Emery definitely did not order this black monstrosity.

"A coat?" Sugar had found this long black puffy coat at the local Salvation Army, and it was toasty warm.

"You look like the Michelin Man," Emery said, wrinkling her nose.

"Correction, a warm Michelin Man." The fitted blue coat Emery had ordered was fine if she was doing something active, but it wasn't warm enough for just walking around town. "Where are you headed?"

"Jen's office. She's letting me interview a few interns there." Jen Lewis was the town lawyer and head of the chamber of commerce. She was also Eric's ex sister-in-law as she was from the Olsson side of The Lodge. Her little daughter, Jessica, and Violet had become fast friends.

Sugar understood Emery's good mood now. Nothing thrilled her more than a new intern. A couple of women their age slowly walked past them. "Hi Sugar," some lady whose name Sugar could not remember said. Sugar didn't miss the fake friendliness when she said her name, and although she couldn't remember who exactly this lady was, she could remember one thing. She was a bitch.

"Hi," Sugar said smiling sweetly as they walked by. The two women had their heads together, whispered something, and laughed.

"Jesus, do people really act like that at our age?" Emery pondered.

"Unfortunately, yes." Sugar had dealt with this way too many times in her twenty-five years.

The kids at school were acting so weird. Sugar had lost count how many times people had stopped talking when she walked up, and then laughed as she walked away. As the day went on, she couldn't help but think they were talking about her.

It was the first week of seventh grade and Sugar had just had a wonderful summer. After Emery's mom had made a deal to make Beatrice into a movie, Sugar and her mother had celebrated by taking an extended European vacation. They had eaten their way through Europe, and Sugar had learned so much about flavors and textures. She couldn't wait to try some of the techniques she had learned from some of the small country bakeries in Italy.

The most exciting thing was she no longer had to take medicine every day. For the first time since she was six years old, Sugar didn't have to take a pill every night before school. Everything would be perfect except she felt like an alien had taken over her body. Puberty had made an appearance that summer, and she nearly reached five foot ten now, towering over the other students.

She had also gone from a training bra to a full C cup. Sugar hugged her notebook to her chest as she walked past a group of eighth grade boys who blatantly leered at them. The boys were acting so weird since she came back.

Once she started taking her medicine and could control her impulses, she had made many friends. She loved physical activity and trying daring stunts, so many of her friends were boys. Her best friend Emery seemed to have gone all boy crazy while she was away, and even though Sugar didn't need medication anymore, most kids with her condition were immature for their age. Sugar was no different, and she was also sensitive. Immature and sensitive were not a good combination for junior high.

She couldn't wait for lunch so that she could see Emery. They had different class schedules as Emery was in advanced placement. Sugar did okay in school, and even though the adults in her life didn't think she was living up to her potential, she didn't care. She was going to be a baker and didn't need all this crap they taught.

"Hey Jeff, wait up," Sugar called when she saw her buddy Jeff walking with some other boys she knew. "Are you going surfing

after school?" Sugar and her mother had moved into a house right on the beach last year, and she loved surfing immediately.

"Are you going to wear the purple wet suit?" asked one of the boys with Jeff that she didn't know well. Sugar felt a blush come to her cheeks. When they had gone surfing the other day, she had almost popped out of her top but stopped it at the last second. Becca had bought her a new one that fit right immediately after Sugar told her about the embarrassing incident.

The other boys snickered. "Cut it out, guys," Jeff said. "Yeah, I'll be at our normal spot." This whole thing had gotten way out of control, and he felt bad about what was being said about his friend.

It was all his fault, but he had needed an excuse when the other boys had seen he was excited when he got out of the water. He didn't know why it had happened. It seemed like it happened all the time now, but with no girls around he didn't want them to think he was gay or something.

By the time lunch rolled around, Sugar was sure people were talking about her. She spotted Emery immediately. Sugar wasn't the only one who sprouted up with summer. Emery was only an inch or two behind her. She watched her grab a table with her new friend, Josh, who was in the advanced placement classes with her. He was fun, and Sugar had liked him immediately when Emery introduced them the first day of school.

"Something really weird is going on," Sugar said as she sat next to Emery and grabbed her lunch out of her backpack.

Emery remained suspiciously silent as she examined her egg salad sandwich intently.

"Emery, do you know what's going on?" Sugar grabbed her friend's arm, forcing her to look at her.

"We'll talk about it after school, I promise." Emery couldn't believe it when she heard the rumors going around school. She

came to Sugar's defense when she heard people talking about it. She was there, she knew it wasn't true, but people didn't want to hear that.

"We'll talk about it now." The pit in Sugar's stomach was growing larger by the second. Something really bad was going on, and it must be much worse than she thought if Emery wouldn't tell her.

Emery sighed. She knew Sugar wouldn't give up until she told her. This was going to hurt her friend, but she had the right to know. "Jeff told people that after you almost popped out of your suit the other day, that you showed him your boobs and let him, well, touch them."

"WHAT?" Sugar shouted. She desperately looked around the large cafeteria. It seemed everyone was looking at them, and people she counted as friends were laughing at her. "Emery, you know that's not true, you were there!"

"I know. I would know it wasn't true even if I wasn't there." Emery looked across the table at Josh, who was playing with his mashed potatoes. "I've told everyone he's lying, right, Josh?"

"She has," Josh confirmed. Sugar was so special. He didn't understand why anyone would do this to her.

"Then why are they still talking about it?" This couldn't be happening. Sugar had been friends with most of these kids since her mom had moved them from LA to San Diego five years ago.

"I don't know." Emery really didn't know why they wouldn't believe her. "It's going to be okay; they'll get bored with it."

Sugar excused herself and went to the bathroom, not wanting to cry in the cafeteria. She wiped her face with some tissue and was about to leave the stall when some girls walked into the bathroom.

"I knew she was a slut." Amanda Miller was one of the reigning mean girls at school and was eating up these rumors about

Sugar Jones. Ever since Sugar had returned from vacation, all Amanda had heard about was how hot Sugar was now, and she was seething with jealousy.

"Emery said it isn't true," said Brittany. She was a friend of Sugar's and didn't want to talk bad about her, but she really didn't want to be on Amanda's bad side. Her friend Heidi elbowed her as Amanda checked her make up in the mirror.

"She's Sugar's best friend, duh." Amanda didn't really believe the rumors either, but she wasn't about to say anything that would stop the momentum. "Sugar always has to be the center of attention." She narrowed her eyes at the two girls. "Don't tell me you're friends with her too?"

"As if," Brittany made the decision in a split second. She didn't want to be the next one on Amanda's hit list. "Maybe her mom needs to check her meds."

"Meds?" Amanda felt like she hit the lottery. "Tell me more," she said as the girls left the bathroom, leaving a completely crushed and heartbroken Sugar in the bathroom stall.

"And I swear I'm going to kill him if he doesn't get me the activity schedule for next month." Emery snapped her fingers in front of Sugar's face. "Are you listening to me?"

"Yes, you are going to kill Alec, the only sibling I like." It was a shot in the dark, but lately when Emery turned murderous, it was because of Alec.

"Fine. I'll just hurt him." Emery had been working nonstop since she first stepped foot in this small town. Between the hotel, the town, Sugar Jones LLC, and the café, she was stretched to her limit. If she wouldn't have been so busy, she would have noticed the sadness seeping out of her friend. Even though Sugar had learned over the years to hide it, Emery could always tell.

Emery happily headed towards Jen's office to find her

next intern as Sugar pulled the door open to the cute little flower shop. Cheeful bells jingled and announced her entrance. Shaking off her mind's previous trip down memory lane, she got back to business. The shop was adorable, and Sugar's eyes went straight to a little arrangement of violets. She would be walking out with that for sure.

She took a deep breath, taking in all the scents that filled the shop. If she closed her eyes, she could almost imagine she was back in warm, sunny California. Flowers always made her happy, and they chased some of those demons away.

It wasn't like she was this damaged individual because she had problems growing up. The one thing Sugar learned in her life was everyone had their struggles. No, all this change and all these new people in her life were making her think of all those bad times. It was almost like a self-preservation system, reminding her that most people she allowed into her heart had hurt her.

A cute redhead was standing behind the register, smiling kindly at an elderly lady who was trying to decide between two different floral arrangements. Sugar browsed as she waited her turn. She had seen the redhead at preschool drop off. If she had to guess, the little boy with the bright red hair was her son, and he was in Violet's class.

The older lady finally decided on a simple bunch of daisies for her friend that was in the hospital. As Sugar approached the register, she sensed the redhead's demeanor change. She was now stiff and formal.

"How may I help you?" she asked without a hint of a smile. She was being polite, but the friendly woman Sugar had just witnessed was completely gone.

"I need an arrangement made for the Snow Globe

Café window." Sugar noticed the flicker of excitement that flashed across the woman's face before she regained her composure. "I'm Sugar Jones," she said as she extended her hand.

"Yes, I think everyone knows who you are." She couldn't keep the sarcasm out of her voice as she shook her hand, and Sugar had now officially reached her bullshit level. With her past experiences still in the back of her mind, she wasn't having this.

"Look, my mother named me Sugar." She placed her hands on her hips and stood tall. "I had my share of taking crap by the time I was ten years old. I don't know what your damage is, but I've done nothing to you."

Guilt flittered across the woman's face. "I'm . . . I'm sorry." She was right. Sugar had done nothing to her to warrant this behavior. "I'm Holly, and my maiden name was Noel, so I know a little about taking crap because of a name."

"I bet," Sugar relaxed a bit. "Look I don't know you, but I have to ask. I'm not stupid. I could see your attitude change immediately when I came in the shop. Why?" Sugar learned over the years that the only way to truly deal with passive aggressive behavior was to confront it head on. She was done with hiding in the bathroom.

The woman had pulled a few books from under the counter. Sugar was distracted temporarily by the photos of beautiful fall arrangements. Holly was really good.

Holly sighed. "I've had my . . . how did you say it . . . share of trouble from the Larssons," she confessed.

"I'm not a Larsson," Sugar reminded her. This was completely confusing. She imagined in a small town like this, a client like The Lodge would keep this place in business. When she asked about who had done the arrangements at the Halloween ball, Alec had told her the shop in town exclusively did their flowers.

She just couldn't imagine someone not liking Alec and Eric. Everyone she met just loved Alec, and Eric seemed well respected by the community at large and was a welcome change from his father. Unless . . .

"I know." Holly felt backed in a corner. She was so stupid and had said too much. It wasn't smart to bite the hand that feeds you and your family. Most people wouldn't have called her out, but even though she just met her, it was clear. Sugar was not most people.

"I just had a lot of problems with Madison back in high school. She practically gave me an ulcer by my junior year," Holly said. "It was a long time ago, and I shouldn't have assumed you would be the same."

"Amanda Miller," Sugar said while she flipped through the pictures. She looked up and saw the confused look on Holly's face. "That's who I had problems with back in high school. By problems, I mean she was the bitch that made it her mission in life to talk shit about me. Sugar's a slut. Sugar's crazy. It was hard to keep up with it all."

Sugar looked up and saw the compassion in Holly's eyes. This girl knew exactly what she was talking about. Emery had her share of bullying, but it was different. She was never the school slut. Emery didn't have boys leering at her, and worse yet, feeling like they had the right to grab at her.

"Same," Holly quietly said.

The bells on the door jingled as a middle-aged woman

walked in. "Sorry I'm late, Holly," she called as she ran to the back of the store.

"I'm sorry, Sugar. I need to run to the store before I pick up Sam. If you like, you can take my book and we can talk about it tomorrow?"

"Do you have anything planned after you pick up your son?" Shit, she was right. It was almost time to pick up the kids. Time had always slipped away from Sugar. This was the first day since she got here that she was getting to pick up Violet without running back to the café. With Becca back in town, Emery, and all her newfound family, it was like she needed to schedule time to see her own kid.

"Just making dinner and fixing a creaking door." Holly said. "Sam's a light sleeper and every time I use the bathroom in the middle of the night it wakes him up."

"I can't help you with the door, but how about you both come to the café after school? You can check out the dimensions of the window, and I have a cheesy chicken casserole ready to go in the oven for dinner." Sugar felt an immediate kinship with this woman. It didn't happen often, but when it did, she couldn't help but act on it.

"That sounds perfect."

☙

"Can't I help you with the dishes?" Holly asked as Sugar carried the last of their plates to the sink in the cute apartment above the bakery.

"Don't even go there. You won't be able to do it right," Emery warned. Sugar was a freak when it came to every aspect of a kitchen.

"I'm good," Sugar said as she flipped Emery off. She

loaded the dishwasher after meticulously rinsing the dishes. Violet had been thrilled to have a friend come over after school, and the two of them were in her room building something with Legos, her favorite toy.

Emery had joined them for dinner, and she seemed to like Holly as much as Sugar did. They had learned that Holly had left Snow Valley when she went to college and returned when she inherited the flower shop from her great aunt.

Sugar rejoined the pair at the dining room table. The ideas Holly had for the window had her brain buzzing with excitement. She really was talented, and Sugar couldn't wait to see the results. Holly confessed to Sugar that it had been on her bucket list to be a part of the window, and Sugar was happy to fulfill that wish.

"Violet is really kind. She asked Sam to play her first day of school." Holly said. "He's so shy and mostly played by himself, but since Violet started school he plays more with the other kids."

Sugar felt such pride for her little girl. She tried to raise her to be empathetic and kind, and it was nice to know it was working. "Thank you. He seems like such a sweet little boy."

"He is," Holly smiled. "He's been having a hard time since his dad has been gone, so having a new friend has meant more than you know. I should have known you weren't like Madison just by how sweet Violet is."

Sugar and Emery learned Holly's husband and walked out on the two of them, leaving Holly to raise her little boy by herself.

Emery snorted. "Why on God's green Earth would you think Sugar was like that pint-sized nightmare?"

Emery and Sugar already had a run in with Madison, and it had not ended well.

"Oh, so you know her?" Holly asked sarcastically.

"Emery called her the help." Sugar knew it was wrong, but after the way her half-sister treated them the first time they met, she couldn't help but smile at the memory.

"You didn't!" Holly would have paid good money to be there for that. "Seriously, you are my new hero."

Emery and Sugar gave Holly the lowdown on the first time they met Madison. They had run into her at The Lodge, and Madison had snootily informed Sugar that she shouldn't get excited because a family trust would guarantee that neither Sugar nor her mother would benefit from the family fortune.

What Madison didn't know was that Becca was wealthy in her own right, and Sugar was on her way. Emery had made the comment that the help shouldn't act like that, and Madison had almost created a family smackdown when she ran to Eric and lied about the situation, making it seem like it was all Sugar and Emery.

"He defended her at first when the school started complaining about her bullying," Holly offered, "but I have to give him credit. When it couldn't be denied anymore, he took care of it."

"I don't like gossip, but seriously, what's her deal?" Sugar had come to a cease-fire with Madison after she defended her against a sexist guest that was staying at the hotel. Madison had offered up a half-ass apology for her behavior and they had come to a tentative peace, but for the most part, they just avoided each other.

"I'm not above gossip at all," Emery said. "Spill."

"She wasn't that bad when we were young." Holly

caught the doubtful look on Emery's face. "Well, not as bad as she became. She could be snotty, but she wasn't downright mean. You do realize that your family is like the town's version of royalty, right?"

Sugar thought about this. It made her uncomfortable, and even with all the help she received last week, she still didn't see them as her family. She just couldn't help that she didn't feel for them what she felt for Becca and Emery. "I guess I hadn't really thought about it," Sugar answered honestly.

Holly craned her neck to make sure the kids were still playing in Violet's room. "I guess that's why I was so nervous when I heard about you, about Violet. My shy kid going to school with a Larsson? I'll admit, it terrified me."

"My child will never act like that." Sugar knew this for certain. Violet had always been sweet, and she would do everything in her power to make sure she never turned into a hateful mean girl.

"Oh, I have no doubt." Holly didn't mean to offend her new friend. "Anyway, Madison was tolerable until high school. We don't have one in Snow Valley, so once junior high is over, we all go to a high school that has kids from all the towns in the area."

"So she wasn't a big fish in a small pond anymore, right?" Emery could see where this was going.

"Yep. Exactly." Holly said. "We were all friends through elementary school and junior high. The kids of Snow Valley break into cliques as soon as they entered high school, and Madison joined the upper echelon."

"She could be a jerk, but she wasn't near as mean as she got when her parents divorced. Then when the news broke that her mom was a lesbian, well things got ugly fast. Madison had zeroed in on me, and she was merciless in her bullying."

"I bet she thought her new friends were going to turn on her," Sugar pondered. No matter how bad things got when she was in school, she wouldn't trade her experience for anything in the world if it meant having friends like that.

"Yeah, I guess. Like I said, her dad had defended her when it was small stuff, but when she turned her wrath on me, it wasn't small stuff anymore."

"Both of my parents worked for her family, so I think she correctly deducted that I wouldn't tell," she continued. "Somehow her dad got a hold of one of her social media rants about me, and it all stopped."

"Did she ever say she was sorry?" Sugar asked softly. She would never get an apology from Amanda Miller. Becca had made sure Amanda Miller had got everything coming to her and then some.

"God, no." Holly couldn't ever imagine Madison saying she was sorry to anyone. "Well, I guess in a roundabout kind of way she has. She's the one that changed over to our shop for all the flowers in The Lodge after I moved back. She doesn't come herself, just sends one of her minions with her directions."

"Well damn, just when I thought we had figured out who the Antichrist was, you had to go and tell us that," Emery said seriously. Holly rolled her eyes, and the three new friends shared a laugh.

After Emery went back to her apartment to get some work done and Holly left to fix her squeaky door, Sugar got Violet ready for bed. It was always her favorite part of the day. Violet would chat about school or her new

friends as Sugar bathed her and put her in her paja-
mas. Soon she would be too old for this, and Sugar was
dreading it.

"In you go," Sugar said as she pulled the covers back.
Violet happily hopped into bed as Sugar tucked her in.
She laid down next to her daughter and Violet cuddled
up to her.

"How are you doing, little monkey?" Sugar asked as
she stroked her hair with her fingers. "Lots of things have
changed. Are you okay with it all?"

"Oh yes, Mommy, I love it here. I love school and
Grandpa and snow and Uncle Alec." Violet thought for
a minute. "I hope we stay here forever. I have my own
room here too!"

"We'll see, okay?" Sugar still wasn't sure this was their
forever place. "Sam's mommy told me you were very
kind and asked Sam to play when he was playing all
alone."

"He's a nice boy and pretty good with Legos." Violet
yawned and rubbed her eyes. It had been a long day.

Sugar hugged her little girl close. "That makes me
very proud of you. We always need to be kind to people,
right?"

"Yes, Mommy," she said sleepily as her eyes started
to close. Sugar laid there for a little bit, listening to her
daughter's breath rise and fall as she drifted off to sleep.

Sugar was raised very modestly by Becca. She hadn't
hit it big with the Beatrice books until Sugar was about
ten, so she remembered living in small apartments and
not getting everything she wanted because they simply
couldn't afford it.

Violet would never have to go without anything.

Between Becca and her grandfather, Violet would be set for life. Sugar knew her daughter, and she really was sweet and kind. She imagined Eric had thought the same thing about Madison at one time. She didn't know how, but she was going to raise this little girl to be grateful and humble. She wouldn't let all of it go to her head.

Maybe it was time to start rewarding her good behavior. A cat over by the Snow Valley Hotel had kittens that were about to be weaned. Even though taking on one more thing seemed crazy, she made up her mind. Violet was finally going to get a pet, and they would go check them out after school tomorrow.

Chapter 4

VIOLET HAPPILY TRUDGED through the snow to the pole barn behind the Snow Valley Hotel. It seemed like once it started snowing here, it just didn't stop. Thor, Jackson's big white Great Pyrenees, trotted beside her, sneaking a kiss or two as Violet giggled with joy.

She had been so very happy when Sugar told her they were going to go pick out a kitten. Sugar could see how it would be easy to spoil her rotten. She wished she could make her that happy all the time, but that wasn't real life. With her recent kind actions and how patient and accommodating Violet had been since the move, she earned this.

They had arrived at the hotel after Violet got out of school to find Alec busy looking through pictures for the new hotel website, with taskmaster Emery cracking the whip. Alec was supposed to complete this assignment days ago, so Jackson volunteered to take them to see the kittens. When they reached the barn doors, he squatted down to Violet's level.

"Now remember, they are just babies, so you have to be gentle," he said. "Their mommy might get mad if she thinks they are being hurt, so you have to be careful."

"I will, Jackson, I promise," Violet said seriously, crossing her heart. "If someone tried to hurt me, my mommy would kick their butt!"

"You're damn right," Sugar said as Jackson chuckled. Normally Sugar was a big stickler on Violet calling adults by their last name. Becca had been that way with her even though most of her friends called adults by their first names, so Sugar had been that way with Violet. After much whining and begging, she finally relented in Jackson's case. Violet had begged a little too.

Sugar felt the chill in her bones subside as they entered the pole barn. The outside was very deceiving; the inside was heated and looked more like a tricked-out man cave than a barn. There was a workbench on one side with various wood projects in different states of completion.

A big flat screen was on the wall, and there were a couple of recliners and an old leather couch in front of it. There was a small kitchenette in the corner. Wood floor stretched across the whole place, and the walls were painted a blue that reminded her of the sea. Sugar imagined the two closed doors were a bathroom and a bedroom.

"Normally girls aren't allowed in here, so you should feel honored." Jackson and Alec both had small studio apartments back at the hotel. Neither one of them were interested in making or caring for a home just yet, but they had built this to have somewhere that wasn't at work. Living where you work is great most of the time, but sometimes you just want to get away.

"I may never get over the thrill," Sugar deadpanned.

"Where are they, Jackson?" Violet looked and looked and didn't see any kittens.

Jackson sighed. "My guess would be my chair." Out of

all the places she could have gone in the big barn, the cat had decided his chair was the perfect place for her new residence. They had homes for most of the new kittens but didn't have any luck locating the mother's home. She had obviously been someone's pet. Jackson and Alec decided to keep her, and once the kittens went off to their new homes, they'd get her fixed.

Jackson plucked the hat off of Violet's head and took her hand as she unzipped her coat. They walked around the set of recliners, and an excited gasp escaped Violet's little mouth.

"Look, Mommy, they are so pretty," Violet whispered. The mother cat was a calico that was mostly white with a few orange and black spots. Four little kittens peeked out from under her. Two of them had taken after their mother, one was an orange tiger stripe, and a noticeably smaller one was gray and black striped.

Jackson sat down on the floor in front of the chair and Violet climbed into his lap. "Hey, Cat." Jackson stroked the mother cat's face, causing her to purr. "My friend Violet here is going to take care of one of your babies."

"Her name is Cat?" Violet asked as she clasped her hands together, unsure if she should touch the little kittens.

Jackson chuckled. "I guess we haven't had time to name her." Curiosity got the best of the kittens and they started coming to the edge of the chair to check out the new visitors, with the little gray runt bringing up the rear.

Sugar squatted down on the other side of the chair. "Gentle now, Violet." Violet reached her little hand out and the kittens began rubbing their little faces against her.

"They like me, Mommy!" Sugar had been worried about being around the mother cat, that she might be anxious to have strangers around her babies. Looking at the cat's face, she stopped worrying. Sugar knew that look. It was a "Get these babies off of me" look that Sugar knew she had those first few months Violet was alive and constantly nursing.

The first three kittens jumped down and Violet clapped her hands excitedly. The little runt stayed on the edge of the chair, unsure about the jump.

Jackson reached over and handed the kitten to Violet. "This little guy was the smallest of the kittens. He still needs extra help."

Violet gingerly cradled the little kitten, cooing and gently petting his head as he snuggled in. "Mommy, can we have this one? He needs extra help."

"I don't see why not." Sugar reached over and pet the little guy's head. She looked up to find Jackson watching her intently, and she gave him a big smile.

One dimple, Jackson counted in his head.

"Did you hear that, Branch, you are coming home with us and I'm going to be your new mommy!" Violet exclaimed.

"Branch?" Jackson asked.

Of course his name would be Branch. Sugar should have seen that coming from a mile away. "There's this little kid movie called *Trolls*. It's Violet's favorite."

"I've seen that movie." Jackson reached over and pet Cat's face. "Maybe we should name her Poppy?"

Violet nodded enthusiastically and gingerly climbed out of Jackson's lap, sitting on the ground with all the kittens.

Sugar looked at Jackson quizzically. "Alec loves that movie," he explained.

Sugar burst out laughing. "Of course he does."

Two, Jackson thought.

"Jackson, these are amazing." With Violet completely entertained by her new animal friends, Jackson was showing Sugar some of his current wood projects. She ran her hand over a beautiful wooden box with ornate fleurs de lis carved into it.

"Thanks. That's going to be my mom's Christmas present. Her mother's side is from New Orleans," he explained. Sugar was impressed that he was thinking about a present for his mother even before Thanksgiving. Becca always said if you wanted to know how a man would treat you, watch how he treated his mother.

"Ah, that must be where your twang comes from." Jackson had a slight accent when he said certain words. Emery, and if she was honest with herself, she, melted when he said her name. Shuugah.

Jackson put his hands on his hips. "I do not twang." He'd been told this before of course, but he still didn't hear it.

Three. "Oh yes you do." Sugar giggled to herself. "If I were a bad friend, I'd tell you what Emery thinks when you say my name, but I'm a good friend," she teased.

"You two are pretty tight." When Sugar and Emery had tracked down Becca a couple of weeks ago, Jackson had observed the two friends when they accidentally stayed at the Snow Valley Hotel, not knowing Sugar's family owned it. They seemed more like family than friends.

"The tightest. Emery and her parents are the only family I have besides my mom." Emery's parents were intellectual and professional, and Sugar couldn't have loved or respected them more. Emery had an older brother and sister, but they had gone to college when the girls were in third and fourth grade.

Once they graduated, they both moved across the country for job opportunities, only coming home for random holidays. They were both doctors, and sometimes Sugar wondered if that's why Emery worked so hard.

"Until now." Jackson stayed out of family business, but he could tell Sugar wasn't accepting her new family with open arms. He cared about them. Alec was his brother in every sense of the word, and Eric had always treated him well, even when it meant issues with John Larsson, Eric's own father.

"Yes, well I don't let people in easily." She set the box down and inspected some long planks of reclaimed wood he was staining in different colors. "I've taken being burned by people to an art form," she said and immediately wanted to take it back. Sometimes her lingering symptoms worked in her favor, and sometimes, like now, they most certainly did not.

"Let me tell you something." He looked right into those beautiful blue eyes. "Knowing what I know, if I could choose anyone to be my long-lost family, it would be them," he said sincerely.

"Understood." These boards really were beautiful and had a lot of character. "How are you going to use these?"

Jackson didn't know Sugar well, but he already learned not to push her. "Once they're all stained, I'm going to piece them together to make a statement wall behind the front desk at the hotel."

"That's going to be quite striking. I love the blue running through some of them." The intimate atmosphere was now non-existent.

"Mommy, I think the kittens are tired," Violet said. All four kittens, plus the newly named Poppy were worn out from playing with her and were snoozing on her lap. Thor kept a watchful eye on the group, proudly lying next to her.

Jackson went over and placed Poppy back in his chair, gently placing the kittens one by one by their mother.

"Are you sure Branch can't come home with us now?" Violet asked hopefully as Sugar zipped up her coat and put her hat back on her head.

"He's not ready to leave his mommy yet, monkey."

"Okay." Violet scrunched her shoulders up. "If he needs his mommy, he needs his mommy."

"What do you say to Jackson?"

Violet reached her arms up and Jackson picked her up. "Thank you for letting me pick my new kitten, Jackson." Throwing her arms around his neck, she gave him a hug and kissed his bearded cheek. "It tickles," she giggled.

"You're welcome. I'll check on him every day, okay?" This really was the sweetest little girl he had ever met.

"Promise?" Violet held her pinky up.

He engulfed her little pinky with his own. "Promise." Sugar smiled at the two, but he couldn't help but notice that there was no dimple.

❧

"Keep your eyes closed," Sugar said as she led her mom from the kitchen to the dining room of the café. Tomorrow was reopening day, and they had an hour before the night shift started. With Violet all tucked in upstairs and Emery working at the kitchen table, now was the perfect time. Sugar had declared the café off limits to her mother ever since she had returned from San Diego, and she was finally showing her the changes.

Paul Anderson had delivered the rest of the tables the day before, and Sugar mentally kicked herself for being disappointed that Jackson hadn't come. She didn't have time for distractions and was well aware that she weirded out on him the other day. It was for the best.

"Oh Sugar, this is silly." Becca had been dying to see the café since she had moved into Eric's cozy cottage in the woods. She had tried to give her space to do her thing, but her patience was up.

"Okay, you can open them."

She was facing the rear of the café and saw that the walls were now butter yellow, which was Becca's favorite color. All the small tables had been replaced by long tables in a gorgeous light pine. The chairs were made of the same wood and had happy ceramic mosaic backs that whirled with color. The gray stone fireplace was alive with flame and polished to an almost impossible shine.

Prints of Sugar's desserts were flat against the walls with no frame. The former storage area had been opened up and had more intimate seating. She slowly turned, not wanting to miss a thing. The floors had been kept the original dark wood, but had been refinished. The contrast with the light wood and walls was striking.

The window had an elaborate arrangement with a huge pumpkin as the centerpiece. Surrounding it were big bunches of flowers in warm fall tones. A random violet poked out here and there, and leaves whirled around the big dome shaped window, dancing in a light that changed from regular, to orange, and then red.

As Becca turned toward the bakery counter, she gasped. She didn't gasp because of the new espresso machines, larger bakery case, or the massive chalk wall with menu items written in ornate calligraphy. No, Becca felt the burn of tears in her eyes when she saw the large photo print of her father and his first wife.

It spanned the entire height of the huge chalkboard menu and would be the first thing people saw when they walked in the door. He was so young, and they were standing in front of the café as workers installed the window behind them. He had his arm casually around her shoulders. Underneath the picture, the lettering said: Lovingly Established in 1947 by Hans and Ingrid Johansson.

She had never seen this picture before. Her mother, Greta, a woman Hans had married later in life after his first wife died, had destroyed them all. She was mentally ill and refused all offers of help. Becca was glad to see Ingrid on the wall as she had worked at this bakery for the first twenty years it was open. Her father loved her very much.

Three smaller pictures ran the length of the photo on the right side. The top one was one of Becca and her father decorating the window for Christmas when she was about Violet's age. The middle one was a picture of Becca with Sugar at Easter, when Sugar was around four years old also. The last one was a picture of Sugar and Violet, taken at a Fourth of July celebration a few months ago.

"I have no words," Becca said as tears ran down her face.

"Mom, don't cry," Sugar said as she embraced her mother.

"I can't help it." She hugged her daughter tightly.

"I'm so touched, so proud. It's perfect, Sugar, absolutely perfect."

Sugar pulled back so that she could look her mom in the eyes. "It's all because of you. You gave me some strong-ass wings, Mama," she said with a slight tremble in her voice.

Becca closed the homemade book she had made for her daughter. She had never thought about writing children's books before, but writing and illustrating this book for her daughter had been the most satisfying project she had worked on since she graduated college.

"What did you think?" This year had been much better than last year, but even with meds, Sugar would still have challenges.

"I liked it, Mama," Sugar said as she cuddled into her mom's side. "So Beatrice struggles when she's a baby so that her wings are strong and she can fly when she's a grown up?"

Becca smiled and kissed the top of her daughter's head. "That's right, sweetheart." She had understood. The idea first came to her when they visited a local museum that had the life span of the butterfly. If you helped the developing butterfly out of its cocoon, it wouldn't be strong enough to fly. She thought this was a perfect lesson for her daughter, but with everything in scientific terms she hadn't understood the message.

Her little girl had plenty of struggles ahead of her. She had felt relief when she was finally diagnosed with ADHD. There was a way to help her. It took three doctors, and the final one, Dr. Lynn, confided in Becca that if Sugar had been a boy, the school probably would have recommended a test back in kindergarten. Girls went terribly undiagnosed because their issues were dismissed as them being ditzy.

They had to try several different medications because amphetamines didn't agree with her. She was a picky eater already, and those type of drugs made her not want to eat at all. They finally landed on a low dosage blood pressure pill medication she could take at night that helped immensely. For the first time in Sugar's short life, she slept through the whole night and could control her impulses much better during the day.

She still had problems at school. The kids remembered the Sugar that constantly interrupted, wouldn't wait her turn, and caused problems during class. Even though her behavior was night and day different from the prior year, the kids were wary of her, so she spent most of her time at school playing alone. A few of the kids had taken to teasing her, calling her owl because of her big eyes.

They stopped when Becca brought it to the teacher's attention, but they still would hoot at her when an adult wasn't around, and other kids had joined in. Sugar was still very sensitive and immature. It hurt her deeply when the kids did this, and after all the research Becca did, she realized her daughter would always be playing catch-up in the maturity department.

The teachers had gingerly brought up that maybe Sugar should be placed in special education classes. It didn't matter that she scored extremely high on the IQ test, or that her behavior had improved. She was labeled here, and Becca didn't see that changing.

She would tell her next week when school was over. They both needed a fresh start, and Becca had found a school in San Diego that was very sensitive to kids with ADHD. The doctor's bills were expensive, and maybe she could get a teaching job down there.

Yes, a change was just what they needed.

Sugar's phone chirped. She broke away from her mom to read the text message. "Emery. It's almost time for me to go live." Sugar was going to go live on several of their social media platforms to announce the reopening of the bakery tomorrow.

"Go ahead, Sug." Becca took another look around. "Your grandfather would love this."

"I'm glad. He needed to be here." Sugar looked at her smiling grandfather and wished she'd had the chance to know him. "Now if some people show up, we'll be in business."

Becca sighed. She wasn't sure whether it happened during those god-awful teen years or after Josh died, but it seemed like whenever things were good, her daughter was too busy preparing for the bottom to drop out to enjoy it. "Of course they will. You'll see."

The two walked arm and arm through the kitchen to the stairs that led to the apartment. "I hope so." After all this work and hiring all these people, Sugar would be devastated if it didn't work out.

❧

Sugar inspected the kitchen with an eagle eye after the day crew had finished their shift. She liked to think she was a fair boss, but she also expected her kitchen to be respected. There was a little flour left on the long marble counter that spanned the length of the kitchen. If it happened again, she'd need to talk to the assistant manager for the day crew.

Considering the week they'd had, Sugar would cut them some slack just this once. She had barely slept the night before they opened, partially from excitement, partially terrified that her massive web presence wouldn't translate to a brick-and-mortar café.

Thankfully she was best friends with Emery, who had convinced her to triple the amount of product to be made for reopening day. The line for the café had wrapped around the entire square by the time they opened. Her employees had put in a lot of overtime keeping up with the demand. Sugar knew it wouldn't be like this forever, but the output of product still would be much greater than it had ever been before.

"You okay over there, monkey?" Violet was sitting at the makeshift table playing on her tablet.

There was a small area separated from the main kitchen by a short partial wall. It had a swinging gate that locked, and Sugar knew that Becca had spent many years perfecting her drawings on that old card table when she was a little girl. Her father always tried to keep her close, but a kitchen could be dangerous for a child. This was the perfect solution.

Violet took after her grandma and loved to draw and color. If Sugar ever got a minute to breathe, she would spruce up the area for her. Sam also liked to draw, and the two of them had already shared a couple of play dates here. Sugar was happy to help out her new friend, whose shop had felt the effects of the town invasion. Holly told Sugar they were doing a crazy amount of sales this last week, and Sugar was glad her success was helping her new friend and all the others in town.

"When can I go play with Branch and Smidge?" she asked. Violet loved being in the café, but since the arrival of her new pets, she wanted to spend more time in the apartment. Somehow Alec had talked Sugar into taking two kittens, and along with the gray and black tabby, she had adopted the orange tiger-striped female.

"Soon, I promise." Sugar wanted to be sure everything was in place when the cleaning crew came tonight. All the small shops in Snow Valley were closed on Sunday. She thought that was ridiculous but was damn grateful for it now. Having a down day enabled the entire café to be deep cleaned once a week, and her employees a set day off.

She was also grateful that she would get to sleep past two in the morning tomorrow. The first episode of *The Holiday Baking Extravaganza* was on tomorrow night, so Monday would be just as crazy as today. As she wiped the wayward flour off the marble counter, and the buzzer for the service door went off.

"It's Jackson! Can I let him in, Mommy?" Sugar's head snapped to the security monitor and her daughter was correct. There stood Jackson awkwardly holding what looked to be a table.

"Go ahead." She tried to ignore how her stomach jumped when she saw him in the monitor. What was he doing here anyway? Surely a bachelor had better things to do on a Saturday night. She hadn't seen him since they went to check out the kittens.

In all honesty, she hadn't seen many people. Emery was in her element, working hard to make the most of the attention the small town was receiving. The Snow Valley Hotel was also reaping the rewards, and Alec and Jackson had been working double time to keep every-thing running smoothly.

Jackson and Violet came into the kitchen. She was clapping her hands and jumping up and down. "Mommy, Jackson made me my own table!"

He was carrying a table made of the same wood as the new café tables, but with just a quick look, Sugar could see the difference. It looked like it had drawers that had *Trolls* characters as handles.

"I meant to have this done when the last of the tables were delivered."

He set the table down outside the little play area. Violet ran to it and opened one of the drawers. "Mommy, it has a King Peppy handle!"

"Is this okay?" he asked the mute Sugar. She nodded as he folded the old card table up and lifted the new table over the small wall. "Oh wait, there's more." He winked at Violet as her mouth dropped open.

"More?" she asked as he laughed and went back outside.

Sugar's hand flew to her heart when he walked in carrying four small chairs. The backs were shaped like violets and filled with the same mosaic pieces used in the chairs for the café. Violet squealed with delight at the sight of them as he placed them around the table.

"I figured you could keep your art supplies in there." Violet was now in awe at the Princess Poppy knob on another drawer.

"Oh, thank you, Jackson!" She engulfed his legs in a big hug.

"You're welcome, sweetie." Jackson patted her head fondly. Who knew that making a kid this happy could bring such joy?

"Mommy, can I go get my crayons?"

Sugar nodded, not trusting her voice. Violet raced up the spiral staircase to get her art bag out of her room.

"I noticed her drawing on that old table when we came by to talk about the other tables," he explained. "I hope I haven't overstepped."

Sugar erased the space between them quickly with her long legs. "The knobs come off and can be changed out when she gets another favorite movie. I made the chairs in the shapes of violets because, well, she'll always be Violet."

Very aware that Sugar was standing very close to him, he looked down and saw all the emotions in her eyes. She put her arms around his neck and pulled him into a full kiss. Snaking his hand around the back of her head, he deepened it, using his other arm to press her body against his.

"Mommy, the kitties are trying to escape!" Violet called through a crack in the door at the top of the stairs. That was Sugar's one rule. The cats could never ever come in the café.

Sugar broke off the kiss. "Thank you." They both tried to regain a normal breathing pattern as Sugar took the stairs two at a time to help her daughter. She shooed the kittens away from the door as Violet happily came down the stairs with her bag.

"Anybody here?" Becca called out from the back door as Sugar descended the stairs. By the time she reached the landing, both her mother and Eric were in the kitchen.

"Grams! Grandpa! Come look at the table Jackson made me!" Violet had dumped her bag on the table, and crayons, colored pencils, and watercolors now dotted its surface.

Eric shook hands with Jackson as he went to examine his work. "Jackson, this is amazing." Eric ran his hand over the King Peppy knob. Just that alone must have taken him countless hours of carving.

"Thanks. Well, I better take off. I left Alec with a group of grumpy new arrivals."

Violet ran back over to Jackson, hugging him once more. "I love, love, love, looooove my new table so much!"

Sugar walked with Jackson to the back door in the big storage room behind the kitchen. "Thank you again. That was a sweet thing to do."

"You kissed me."

Sugar's hand flew to her mouth. "Oh Jackson, I'm so sorry. I've been wanting to do that all week and have trouble with my impulses sometimes. It won't happen again."

Here he was, doing something nice for her kid and she had jumped him. Sugar had heard all about Jackson since she'd been in town. He didn't get involved with women who had children, and now she had put him in an awkward position.

"That's not what I meant," he started to say as Violet's voice rang out through the air.

"Mommy, come see! It has Bridgette too!" Sugar squeezed his hand and gave him a big smile as she walked away. He was too dumbfounded to even count the dimple.

I've wanted to do that all week was playing through his mind as he headed back to the hotel. Who was this woman and what was she doing to him?

Chapter 5

"ARE YOU SURE YOU WON'T change your mind?" Emery wanted to set up an event in town for everyone to watch the first episode of *The Holiday Baking Extravaganza* that night.

The two friends were finishing up a meeting with their Sugar Jones team. Sugar felt bad for having it on a Sunday, but it couldn't be helped. Until the café was stable, things would have to be this way. She hadn't been this surprised at the span of their reach since that very first video went up ten years ago. People may say that streaming was the future, but for now, television was still king.

Even without it airing, she received some offers from The Food Network for some of their competition shows. This was all going incredibly fast. Normally Sugar loved fast, but everything all together was making her feel overwhelmed. Emery was thrilled, but Sugar needed a minute to breathe.

"Yes, I'm sure." Sugar didn't want to make a huge deal about it. She was plain tired, and if she was honest, a little worried about how she would come across on TV. "Just like I told my mom, you are welcome to watch it with Violet and me tonight, but I just want to stay home."

Her mom and Eric both wanted to have a small party for her at the big house on The Lodge's property, but she declined. Becca knew when not to push. Violet, missing the water sports back in California, was currently with them swimming in the big Olympic-sized pool at the luxury resort, giving Sugar a few hours to concentrate on her team.

Sugar couldn't wait until things calmed down and she could be the one swimming with her daughter. She felt for those mothers who had to drop their kids off at daycare for eight hours a day, every day. That would drive Sugar insane. Even though she was busy, a small part in the back of her mind still worried about her daughter during the five hours she was at preschool.

"Okay, okay." Emery closed her laptop on the table that had become her new office.

"Besides, I need to stay away from Jackson for a while after kissing him yesterday." Distance would ease the awkwardness. She couldn't avoid him forever, but she could stay away from him until it wasn't weird anymore.

"WHAT?" Emery had been with Sugar for hours. "We've been together all afternoon and you are just now telling me this?"

Sugar shrugged her shoulders and went into the kitchen to get more coffee with Emery hot on her heels. Coffee. That's what she needed.

Emery had seen the table he'd made for Violet, and it didn't take much to piece together what happened. Like Becca, she had put two and two together. Sure, the man might like Violet, but someone who put that much care and time into a project must like the mother an awful lot too.

She pulled herself up on the counter and watched Sugar make another pot of coffee. "Details. I need details."

"There isn't much to say. He brought the table, Violet was thrilled, ran upstairs to get her crayons, I jumped him, Mom and Eric showed up, he left."

"They caught you?" Emery said, intrigued. She had been sorely deprived in the romance department.

"No, nothing like that. Violet ran to get her crayons, and she couldn't get back downstairs without letting one of these monsters out." Sugar shooed Smidge off the counter. These cats were going to drive her insane. "It brought me to my senses when she called down the stairs. Mom and Eric showed up, and I walked him to the door and apologized and said it wouldn't happen again."

Emery begged off Sugar's offer of coffee and followed her back into the living room. "You apologized? Do you really think he didn't want you to do that? What did he say?"

Sugar sat in what was now her favorite chair, pulling her ever-present quilt over her. "Em, he was being nice to my kid. I don't think he said anything. I just got the hell out of dodge as soon as I said I was sorry." Both cats jumped in her lap, purring their little hearts out.

"How can you be this clueless?" Emery said. "I know you don't have a ton of experience with men, but good God are you blind?" One of the kittens noticed Emery's bangle bracelet and jumped to the couch to attack.

"It doesn't matter, Em, it can never happen."

"Is he a bad kisser or something?" Emery shook her arm as the little kitten batted at her bracelets.

"Oh no, it was hot." Sugar didn't want to think about how hot it was. She stroked Smidge, who had decided Sugar was her person.

"Then why?"

Sugar shook her head. "How many reasons why do you want? Our families are intertwined. A casual thing would not work out."

"So why would it have to be just a casual thing?"

After getting to know Jackson, even Sugar thought the two of them would be a perfect fit. He didn't seem to be a social butterfly, was incredibly active, and couldn't care less what people thought.

"Emery, we both know I'm not good at relationships."

Emery swatted the little kitten away when it started playing rough. "What are you talking about? You're fine with relationships."

"If Josh were here, I'm sure he'd disagree," Sugar said more to herself.

It was rare for her to bring up Josh, so Emery jumped on it. "If Josh were here, he would have realized what an idiot he was being by now."

Sugar played with her long blonde hair, braiding the ends. "We made pies on the show tonight. I think we should offer them in the café, but I'm not sure how long."

Every time they started talking about Josh, she would change the subject. Emery was done. "No Sugar, we aren't changing the subject."

Sugar felt that lump in her throat that she hated so very much. Grief was a funny thing. It never went away, you just learned to deal. Her way of dealing was acting like it wasn't there. "The past is the past. We can't change it, so why talk about it?"

"Because I need to talk about it!" Emery was so tired of this. "Maybe if I'd kept my big mouth shut, he'd be alive." There, she said it.

Emery was shaken from sleep by a pounding on her door. She looked over at her clock. Dear God, it was three in the morning. Grabbing her robe, she opened the dorm door before he woke up the whole hall. She didn't have to ask who it was. She'd bet her life it was Josh and he was drunk. Again.

How he got past the front desk after curfew was anyone's guess, but charming people had never been Josh's problem. Not for the first time she wondered if maybe he had developed a serious problem. This had gone past the normal frat boy drinking. If she was honest with herself, it was past that for a while now.

"What the hell, Josh!" She ushered him inside. Emery knew she would be getting complaints again.

"Emery!" He opened his arms up wide and swept her off her feet in a giant bear hug.

"Put me down right now." This was happening more and more since Sugar started working the night shift at a popular bakery. "Are you wasted again?"

Josh plopped down on the bean bag in the corner of Emery's room. She couldn't count how many times over the last three years he had slept there. Josh had been thin most of his life, but Emery couldn't help but notice how puffy he looked. Normally he was handsome in a geeky sort of way, like Clark Kent, but now he looked bloated and red faced.

"You sound like Sugar now," Josh said in an accusatory tone. "If she didn't work that job, I wouldn't have to come here. I don't feel like being alone."

Emery retrieved a water from her small apartment sized refrigerator and tossed it to him. Sugar was going to be furious when she got home. "So this is Sugar's fault?"

Ever since they started college, this had become an increasingly common occurrence. When Sugar went to Paris, things got really bad, but Emery thought they were getting better. Worry filled her as she waited for an answer. Of course it would be Sugar's fault. Everything was Sugar's fault when he was drunk.

"She doesn't need to work there. It's like she doesn't want to be around me. Well she's stuck with me now, isn't she?"

"Josh, blaming Sugar for everything is getting old." Emery grabbed the bottle he was fumbling with and opened it for him. "She's there to learn. She's never worked in a Jewish bakery before."

Laughter bubbled from Josh's throat as he took a drink. "Maybe I should tie something shiny around my neck. That might keep her attention."

Emery didn't know this stranger. This was not the sweet, goofy, caring Josh she had been best friends with for eight years. She knew he'd be back tomorrow, full of apologies. "That's cruel, Josh."

"But true. We wouldn't be in this situation if she could concentrate for more than two seconds." Josh gulped down his water.

Pulling the small desk chair out, Emery sat down and rested her arms on her knees. She was tired in every sense of the word. "That would have happened to anyone and you know it."

Sugar's mom, Becca, had been in a car accident up in LA, and Sugar had flown up there immediately. Refusing to leave her mother's side, she forgot to take her birth control pills with her. Becca was banged up but fine, and Sugar missed enough days that her birth control wasn't effective anymore.

After being on pills most of her young life, Sugar wanted to look into different options before going back on a pill, so they had to use condoms while she weighed the options that didn't include a daily pill. Josh hated it.

"Yes, Sugar is perfect and I'm an asshole."

Emery reached over and whacked him. She didn't know why she bothered. He would claim to not remember any of this tomorrow. "Grow up, Josh. No really, grow up. You're going to be a father and these drunken episodes need to stop."

Josh leaned forward and grabbed Emery's hand. "Want to know a secret?" he whispered.

"No, Josh, I do not want to know a secret." She snatched her hand from his. Tomorrow she needed to have a serious talk with Sugar. This was completely out of hand. Emery couldn't deny it anymore; Josh had a problem.

Ignoring her, he continued on. "Remember when we went to Vegas for that conference a couple months ago? Sugar and I partied our asses off."

"Anyway, when we got back to the room, we were way gone. She allegedly can't remember shit, but she remembered to ask me to use a condom. Funny how she pulls that excuse out when she needs it."

Searching for her phone, Emery knew Josh would be going nowhere tonight, and she needed to let Sugar know where he was. She only hoped he hadn't driven here.

"So I figured, what the fuck? She wouldn't know if I didn't use one," he snorted. "Whoops."

Emery stared at Josh like he was a stranger. How many times had she listened to him complain about Sugar's pregnancy being all her fault?

"Did you drive here?"

"No, I walked. I'm drunk, not stupid, Emery."

Emery just wanted to beat the hell out of him. She wasn't stupid either, and she couldn't watch her friend be treated like this anymore. "Then walk your ass home, I'm done."

"Oh, come on, Em. Don't be like that."

"Get the hell out, Josh." Emery needed to tell Sugar this, and she didn't know what the fallout would be. She had personally seen Josh make Sugar feel like crap about the pregnancy, and the whole time he knew it was his own decision that caused it.

"That's bullshit and you know it." After much begging,

Sugar had gone with Emery to a few Al-Anon meetings after he died. She didn't know if he was an alcoholic before he passed away, but he definitely was on his way if things didn't change.

The one thing she learned was you couldn't change someone who didn't want to be changed. The meetings were actually helping, and then one of the bitches from high school walked in one night and Sugar walked out. Even though she didn't have contact with any of those girls for years, but she still couldn't ber the thought of giving one of them ammunition against her.

"Why is it bullshit? Huh? Telling you about that set everything in motion. You never trusted him again, and he knew it."

"Em, you did the right thing by telling me. How many times did he crack jokes about me forgetting my pills?" Sugar pulled the blanket tighter over her shoulders. He would always claim to be joking when she got upset, but she knew he wasn't.

Emery got up and pushed Sugar over, sliding into the chair next to her. "Then why do you think it's your fault?"

"Because I never should have started things back up with him." Sugar rested her head on Emery's shoulder, suddenly so very tired. When she went to Paris for two semesters, they hung in there the first semester, but the constant late-night calls usually pertaining to how selfish Sugar was for going just got to be too much. She broke up with him after the New Year.

Sugar had never admitted this before, and Emery was shocked. "You wanted your friend back."

She shook her head yes, not trusting her voice. Sugar

knew Josh didn't sit around and wait. He made his way through the female population at school.

He treated her so badly during that time, and it was practically impossible to have Sugar Jones LLC meetings. When she finished her internship and came back to California, Josh begged her to take him back. Sugar finally relented.

Wiping a wayward tear from her cheek, Sugar cleared her throat. "I wasn't in love with him anymore. I love him, I'll always love him, but not like that."

"We grew up and he didn't." Emery wiped away her own tears. "I always blamed his behavior on being some crazy frat boy. I should have known better."

"Who doesn't act like that in college?" How many people had Sugar known who acted exactly like Josh?

Emery rested her head on Sugar's. "But with his family history, and how out of control he got, I should have known." Josh's father was an alcoholic, and the rest of the family acted like it was perfectly normal.

"He was good at hiding it." After he died, Sugar had found airport bottles of booze hidden everywhere. "Maybe I should have left him when you told me what he did. He promised he would scale down the drinking, but he never did. He just hid it then."

"It all would have been so much easier if he was just a jerk all the time," Emery said.

"I know. He'd do something stupid and be back to himself for weeks until it happened again." Sugar couldn't stop the tears now. All the years of holding it in was like a crack in the dam, and it was pouring out now.

"I'll never forget the look on the police officer's face when she saw I was pregnant," Sugar continued. "I can barely remember anything else from that night, but I'll always remember the crushed look on her face when she realized she had to tell this young pregnant woman that her husband was dead."

"I don't want Violet to ever know how he died." Sugar started pulling herself together. Above all, she knew this. Sugar and Emery made a vow never to tell anyone, not even Becca.

Keeping secrets was a funny thing. People would know something they wanted to share, or it was so juicy, they'd share it with someone they thought they could trust, who would turn around and do the same thing. Before you knew it, lots of people knew. Emery and Sugar had experienced something similar in the past, so they would always say "Take it to the grave" when under no circumstances was something to be repeated.

"Of course not, but she can know the good Josh, the Josh we loved."

Sugar thought about that. She would love for her daughter to know the sweet, kind boy who made her feel safe when boys didn't make her feel safe at all.

"I miss that Josh, so much. I kept thinking he'd come back." Sugar felt like a small weight had been lifted off her chest.

"Me too. He would have, you know, come back." Emery was sure of it. "He wouldn't have treated Violet like his father treated him."

"I think so too." They would never know, but it was something both women needed to believe.

Chapter 6

"MOMMY, HURRY, it's about to start!" Out of all the people in the room, Violet was the most excited. Not only was her mommy on TV, but she was getting to stay up an hour after her bedtime.

Emery had gone back to her apartment to give Sugar some space after their talk, but now she was back. She wouldn't miss this for the world. Becca and Eric had brought Violet home, and Alec tagged along to watch the show.

"Do we have to watch this?" Sugar whined as she brought big bowls of popcorn into the room.

"Yes!" the room answered in unison.

Most of the show contestants were professionals, but they would usually have a home baker or two mixed in with the nine of them. In all the years she had watched, Sugar only knew of one time that a home baker won.

The host, Tyler Smith, was a childhood star once upon a time and was still cute as ever. Sugar liked him immediately. Breaking the child-star-gone-bad stereotype, he lived a good life and always had his kids running around the set. With striking green eyes and dark hair, he wasn't bad to look at either. He still had it going on at thirty.

The studio was decked out in the colors of fall with a giant arrangement of gourds in the center of the studio. "Welcome to The Holiday Baking Extravaganza!" Tyler opened his arms wide, his movie-star smile beaming at the camera. "Let's meet our contestants!"

Emery squealed, actually squealed. "I can't believe you met Tyler," she sighed. They were all gathered around watching the big TV over the fireplace. Becca and Eric were cuddled up on the couch, and Alec took over Sugar's favorite chair. Sugar, Emery, and Violet sat on the floor like they did for so many years before.

"He's really nice too," Sugar said.

"Overrated." Alec said. "I never understood why all the girls in high school were so head over heels for him."

"Jealousy is the best form of flattery, they say," Emery pointed out. The host introduced the nine contestants one by one, each of them giving a little bio. This show definitely had a formula, and you could almost guess the personalities before they came on.

"I'm Jasmine and I loooooooooooove Christmas!" In the confessional booth Jasmine told the audience about herself, punctuated by giggles. She had on giant reindeer earrings and a necklace that lit up with Christmas lights. "I'm an executive pastry chef from Long Island, and I'm thirty years old."

Jasmine's outfit came to life as lights flashed all over her ugly Christmas sweater. "I'm fluffy, large, and in charge!" She was a beautiful larger woman with striking cheekbones and a friendly smile.

"That's such bullshit," Sugar said. "They told her to act like that." Jasmine had a biting sense of humor and probably had the least amount of Christmas spirit out of them all. Sugar bonded with her immediately and still talked to her.

There were always four people who didn't get much attention, and you knew they would be the nameless faces that were voted off the first two shows.

There was also the chauvinistic man named Bob who made stupid comments, the southern grandma named Marge, and the young buck named Jared who went over the top with everything. Sugar was supposed to be the ditzy blonde, but they got a shock once she started the show.

The room erupted in applause as Sugar came on the screen.

Her hair was pulled back in an elaborate updo that called back to the Romans, and she had on a soft blue fitted sugarjones.com shirt. With her winged eyes, highlighted cheekbones, and full lips that were painted pink, she looked more like a movie star than a chef.

"I'm Sugar Jones, and I'm a classically trained pastry chef and social media personality," she said with a large eye roll. No amount of coaching could get Sugar to act the way they wanted her to act.

The screen cut to a picture of Sugar standing in front of the large snow globe window of the café. "I just started running a café that's been in my family for fifty years, the Snow Globe Café in Snow Valley, Colorado," she said in a voiceover recorded just a few days before.

"I don't know how you talked them into doing that," Sugar said to Emery as the room shushed her.

"I'm a widow and I have a four-year-old daughter named Violet." The screen cut to a picture of Sugar and Violet decorating Christmas cookies, Violet's face blurred out.

Back in the confessional booth, Sugar leaned forward and rested her arms on her knees. "You are going to blur her face, right?" The producer answered in the affirmative in the background. "Good. A four-year-old is not old enough to decide if she wants to be a public figure."

"Mommy, why'd you do that?" Violet pouted as Sugar hugged her.

"I'm here to prove I have actual chops. People know I can make beautiful desserts, and now they'll know they are delicious too."

The screen cut back to the kitchen, the contestants lined up behind their workstations. "Here's how it works. There are two challenges every week. You'll know what both of them are so you can work on round two during round one, but don't waste too much time. One person will be eliminated after each round, so make sure that round one dish will keep you here," Tyler said.

"Today we would like you to first make two different kinds of mini pies." The camera panned to the contestants showing different emotions, from nervous to excited. "We want you to stretch your creative muscles, so make sure they're fantastic."

Back in the confessional, Jasmine giggled. "Two pies in two hours? Why? Why?" She shook her fists to the sky.

Bob appeared in the confessional. "Is this competition for kids? Simple. No one can touch me."

"The holidays are all about sharing, so for your second challenge, you must make a dish meant to be shared. It can be sweet or savory, but it must be baked." The camera focused directly on Tyler's handsome face. "You'll have two hours for the first challenge, and two hours for the second. There will be one hour of rest time between the two."

The contestants' workstations were lined up in front of Tyler. Everyone was getting ready to run. "Give me five!" Tyler pointed at a big countdown clock above the giant gourd *arrangement. Tyler counted down to five and a loud buzzer went off.*

The participants ran to the large pantry in the back of the room with large baskets to gather their ingredients. With her long legs, Sugar reached it first, and with a determined look of concentration began gathering her ingredients.

"They told us what we would be making a couple of hours before the show started," Sugar told the group. She had her entire time planned before they even entered the studio kitchen.

A few more people had their introductions and Tyler started interviewing people about what they would be making.

Tyler walked up to Sugar, who was pouring brandy into a batch of cranberries boiling on the stove. "I noticed you used frozen cranberries. Will that make a difference?"

"It makes a big difference, Tyler." Sugar gave her cranberries a big stir and tasted them with a small spoon. "Always use frozen. They freeze them right after they're picked, and fresh can get an almost medicinal taste if they aren't used immediately."

"What are you making . . ." Tyler started to ask as Sugar ran back to the refrigerator section to get her pie crust that was resting. He looked at the camera and smiled, shrugging his shoulders. "Alrighty then."

The contestants all worked diligently. Some of their workstations looked like a grocery store blew up. Jared, the young contemporary chef, couldn't get his smoking gun lit, so Sugar helped him.

Back at her station, Sugar had put her pie crust over an ice cube tray and was meticulously making indentations in each of the holes. "Hey blondie, you know you can't put those in the oven, right?" Bob the jerk smirked. *Of all the people in the competition, Sugar had to be next to him.*

Sugar kept making her indentations but raised one arm in the air, a pixelated finger facing Bob.

"Sugar!" Becca shook her head. The room shushed her as Sugar came into view in the confessional.

"My mother is going to kill me," Sugar told the audience. "How long did I last?"

"About fifteen minutes," the producer said offscreen.

A beep came across the screen as Sugar's mouth was blurred, but obviously saying "Shit."

Sugar sat up straight and clasped her hands, folding them in her lap. "Sugar," she said, doing her best Becca impersonation. "Sweetheart, this is a family show for the holidays. Please don't use profanity."

She leaned in to the camera. "Want to know something? Geniuses curse a lot. I read it in an internet meme, so it must be true," she said with a sly smile and a wink.

Sugar dodged as Becca leaned over to whack her.

"He deserved it," Alec said. "What an ass."

"You have no idea. He's terrible." Everyone involved with the show couldn't stand him. They had cut a bunch of stuff the jackass said to Sugar during that first challenge. He was lucky this was all they showed.

"Time's running out, bakers. You should be plating," Tyler said as the contestants were whipped up in a frenzy. Sugar was kneading dough, her blues eyes staring at the clock. All her desserts were plated for the competition, and she was trying to get dough for the next round done.

"You finished ahead of time," Tyler said, obviously impressed. "What is this?"

"It's an enriched dough for round two, but it needs at least an hour and a half to rise. If I can get it in the drawer before time, I'll be golden."

Tyler started counting down from ten as Sugar slapped her dough in a bowl, covered it with plastic wrap, and slammed it into the proofing drawer just as time was called. She wiped her forehead with the back of her hand and let out a breath.

"Let's meet our judges!"

A regal older woman with silver hair in a high bun walked out. She was dressed impeccably in a black blazer and trousers, with a soft tan shirt underneath. An elaborate turkey brooch adorned her lapel.

"Bettie Hogan is a chef, cookbook author, and has been telling us how to live with style for over fifty years."

A handsome man in his late twenties came into view. With dark brown hair and deep brown eyes, he was the reigning celebrity chef heartthrob. He had only been on the show for a couple of years, and Sugar always wondered why. He didn't seem to have any holiday spirit and didn't particularly like sweets.

"Hunter Solomon is a chef, restauranteur, cookbook author, and television personality from New York City."

The next judge appeared. He was the only one that didn't make Sugar feel like a giant. It was funny how people on TV seemed so much taller when you're watching them. He was a middle-aged African American man with rich mocha skin and dark, soulful eyes.

"From across the pond, we have Harry Wilson. He has bakeries all over the world and has won the James Beard award twice."

Out of all the judges, Harry was the nicest. He was fair and gave constructive criticism. Harry could tell you your dish sucked, and you'd still want to have a beer with him.

The contestants lined up in front of the judges. One by one they presented their dishes to be scrutinized.

When it was Sugar's turn, she stepped in front of the judges, her two dishes sitting in front of them.

"Today I've prepared cranberry mini pies with a swiss meringue leaf." Small bites made from the ice cube tray surrounded a beautifully piped leaf of meringue that was partially died red with cranberry juice and toasted, giving it a nice fall color.

"Is that thyme I'm tasting in the crust?" Harry asked.

"Yes, there's thyme in the crust and brandy and spices in the cranberries."

"Smart. The sugar from the meringue cuts through those very tart cranberries. Good job."

"Thank you," Sugar said with a huge smile.

"The presentation is stunning," Hunter said. "Almost as pretty as you."

The camera panned to Sugar, who looked uncomfortable but gave him a nod.

"What does that have to do with anything?" Bettie snapped. "Sugar, this is a very creative way to present your dish, and it is delicious, but watch your salt level. Just a pinch more salt and this would have been perfect."

Sugar presented her second dish, a chocolate cream pie, to more good comments, and rejoined her fellow contestants. Bob was declared the winner of the round with Sugar in second, and a nameless face from Atlanta was sent packing.

Jasmine shook her head in the confessional. "How did that happen? The girl obviously survives on carrots!"

"What the hell!" Sugar exclaimed. Jasmine and she were cool. Her phone vibrated and she looked and saw it was Jasmine.

"They told me to say that," the text message read. Sugar was about to type back, "But you didn't have to" but decided to just ignore it.

After being on the show, Sugar experienced the producer's promptings also. They were trying to craft a story, and all the people were supposed to check a box. Most of the contestants were there because they wanted to follow the path of being on television, and Sugar didn't. She refused to check her box, and the producers didn't have a clue what to do with her.

Sugar was preparing to roll out her dough for her Swiss tea ring. Instead of the normal sweet filling, she was giving it a savory makeover with sausage and spices normally found in stuffing. After the first round, the judges stayed on set and would periodically talk to the contestants.

"Where did you learn about dough?" Bettie asked as she watched Sugar lean down to smell the dough and gently tap it with her finger. The judges had joined Sugar now, and while she may have run away from Tyler earlier, she couldn't do that to them.

It was perfect. She dumped it out of the bowl onto her floured workstation and prepared to roll it out. "My mom. Her dad was a baker, but he died before I was born. She taught me all his recipes when I was young."

"I thought as much. They don't teach techniques like that in culinary school."

The screen cut to Sugar in the confessional. "My mom, well she's just everything. She's my hero. I had a lot of challenges growing up, and she never gave up on me, always believed in me. She's the reason I'm here, and to do good with one of my grandfather's recipes would mean the world to me."

"Oh sweetheart," Becca said as she scrambled out of Eric's arms and joined her on the floor, engulfing Sugar and Violet in a big hug.

"It's the truth."

"It's money," Emery said and grinned sheepishly as Sugar threw a pillow at her. Sugar had been so sincere, so heartfelt. "Hey, America is going to eat that up with a spoon."

Any doubts Sugar had about how she would be portrayed evaporated. The show was giving her the good edit.

ෆ

The judges loved Sugar's tear and share Swiss tea ring, and after some more flirting by Hunter that caused more admonishment from Bettie, Sugar was declared the winner of the round. Everyone left the apartment extremely proud of Sugar.

Emery was going back home for the week to spend Thanksgiving with her family. Sugar and Violet would be spending Thanksgiving at the big house on The Lodge's property, which Sugar thought was ridiculous. Here she was a chef and she wouldn't be cooking on Thanksgiving, the biggest food holiday of the year. Becca had insisted, so she finally relented.

Sugar was tucking Violet in for the night. "What did you think of the show, monkey?"

"I thought it was really, really good. You helped that man with the smoker thingy. That was nice," Violet said with a yawn.

Kids really did pick up on everything. "I suppose it was. We always have to try and be kind, right?" Then and there, Sugar decided to try a little harder not to use her colorful vocabulary around Violet. Yes, kids needed to learn that adults did things that they couldn't, but she needed to set a better example in that area.

"Yes, Mommy. Are you going to read me a story?" she asked while cuddling up to her mother.

"It's way past your bedtime. How about I tell you a story?"

Violet yawned again. "About what?"

Remembering her conversation with Emery earlier, Sugar decided it was time to tell her little girl more about her father. "How about why I named you Violet?"

Violet shook her head enthusiastically. She had never heard this one before.

"Once upon a time there was a girl named Sugar. She had a bad day at school, so one of her very best friends brought her some flowers to cheer her up. His name was Josh."

"My daddy?" Violet asked in a sleepy voice.

"Yes, your daddy." Sugar brushed the hair from Violet's forehead and continued. "So Josh was very kind, and he thought the violets looked cheerful, so he brought Sugar violets. They fell in love and Josh would always give her violets for special occasions, or when he was in trouble."

Violet giggled and Sugar closed her eyes, calming herself. She could do this.

"So Josh was in an accident and went to heaven, so he couldn't be there when Sugar had their baby. Sugar knew that he would want to be there so very much, and she was sad because she knew Josh would have brought her violets."

Sugar took a deep breath and gained control of the lump in her throat. "Then she had a great idea. Their baby was the most cheerful, beautiful baby in the world, so if she named her Violet, Josh would be able to give her violets every day for the rest of her life."

"I like that story, Mommy," Violet said as she started to fall asleep.

"Me too," Sugar said. She managed to hold the tears until Violet fell asleep, and as she left the room she felt as if another weight had been lifted. This would be easier next time.

CR

Jackson threw his phone and keys onto the small table next to his bed in the plain but comfortable room. He took off his shirt and headed to the small bathroom. Both he and Alec lived in the small hotel, and if things kept going the way they were, they'd need to make different living arrangements. They had been booked solid since the first snowfall, and they justified living there because they had empty rooms.

You're just tired, he thought to himself. One of his favorite distractions was a few towns over for a short skiing holiday, and he told her he was too busy with work to hook up, and then he logged out of Tinder. Focus on the hotel was important now, and he tried to convince himself that was why, not a certain baker.

Hiring Emery had been the smartest thing they did, and she'd taken their social media accounts to new heights. With virtually no advertising budget, Snow Valley Hotel was booked almost the entire season and had a wait list.

Sugar's popularity with the café and the attention she brought the town didn't hurt either. He just wondered how much more things would grow now that the show was airing. They played it in the large common room, and Jackson took over duties as host so Alec could go watch with his sister.

She was amazing. Jackson never saw her so carefree, so alive as she acted on the show. It was puzzling, considering most people would be more reserved and probably scared to death to be in a contest like that. Nothing about that woman made a damn bit of sense.

On the show she looked different too. He liked her more natural day to day look, but the va-va-va-voom thing she had going on wasn't half bad. Several of the hotel guests had whistled when she came on screen, and he wanted to punch them.

She kissed him.

He sighed as he brushed his teeth. The thought he tried desperately to keep out of his mind kept cropping back up, no matter how hard he tried to squash it. He'd heard people say things like they felt it in their toes when they kissed someone. Jackson always thought that was crap, but now he knew it was real.

Dear God, she apologized for it, like she took advantage of him or something. He was a most willing participant. *I've wanted to do that all week* was on constant repeat in his head since it happened, and he didn't know how to shut it off.

Jackson tried to be a good man, so he didn't mess with women with children. It didn't matter if he was honest up front about his desire to stay single. People could still get attached, and it wasn't fair to the kids. He hoped one day he'd make a great husband and father, but he didn't want those things now. Violet was a precious little girl and deserved someone in her life who would be interested in taking over that role since she didn't have a dad.

It won't happen again. She actually said that. He plopped down on his bed, exhausted. The thought of it never happening again was unimaginable, and despite his internal struggle, deep down he knew he would be doing everything he could to make sure it did happen again.

ೞ

"I said no, Emery." Sugar was racing around the living room and kept coming in and out of view on Emery's tablet.

"Sugar, just stop for a minute!" Emery said. "You're making me dizzy."

"Violet, find your boots!" Sugar called as she sat down for a second. "I'm late, Emery. I know, shock, surprise, but my mom is going to kill me if I'm late for Thanksgiving."

Emery leaned closer to her screen. "Listen to me, Sugar, we need to jump on this."

Sugar sighed. All this attention since the show aired last Sunday was unwanted and exhausting. She'd done it again, jumped into something spur-of-the-moment without thinking about the consequences.

"I'm not going to hock some dishes for a big box store."

"Grrrrrrrrrrrrr, you are driving me crazy!" Emery wanted to reach through her tablet and strangle the girl. "You are going to design a line of baking dishes and serving plates. Don't even tell me you aren't interested in that."

"I'm not."

"This is what we've been working for all these years! Sugar, this is a level even I never dreamt could happen."

Sugar glanced at her phone as a text came through. *You better be out that door in ten minutes, missy,* Becca texted.

"That's what you and Josh worked for. I never cared about the money." Josh had come from a middle-class background and hated it. He was bound and determined to be as wealthy as his classmates in school. He was there on a scholarship because he was highly intelligent, and although he wanted for nothing growing up, he always felt like his childhood was lacking.

"Sugar, it is easy to say that when you are well off," Emery pointed out. "I thought you would be over this whole 'I hate the rich' stuff now that you found out the real story about Eric."

This was going nowhere. "Listen, how about this. When you get back in town next week, I promise I'll go over the proposal with you and give it a fair shake. Deal?"

They ended their call with Emery placated for now. Violet stood in the living room holding her boots. "Mom, I don't want to wear these. They don't go with my pretty dress!"

Mom. This last week Violet decided that she was a big girl now and Sugar would now be known as Mom. There was nothing like your own child stabbing you in the heart.

Violet looked pretty as a picture in her lilac dress with beautiful violets embroidered around the neckline and cascading down the skirt. Her long blonde ringlets were pulled back from her face with a violet-covered headband. She looked like a kid. She didn't look like a baby, or a toddler, but an actual child. How did her mother make it through all this?

The dress looked more like she should be going to a wedding, not a family holiday. Becca had bought the dress, along with one for Sugar. Apparently, the Larsson family holidays were incredibly formal. All her life Sugar dreamt of a big family holiday. Standing there in this fitted blue dress, sweatpants and cooking and eating until they were positively stuffed, seemed better and better.

"I have our shoes to wear in the house in this bag." Sugar desperately looked around the living room and produced the shoes. "Let's roll, kid, or Grandma is going to kill me."

◯Ꝛ

They arrived at the big house on The Lodge's property. The big house was a mini version of The Lodge, all rich polished wood and fancy chandeliers. It was gorgeous but cold, not homey at all. Sugar couldn't imagine growing up in a house like this.

People milled around the large living room mingling and having cocktails. Sugar met most of these people during the short time that she lived here. Most had come to the café and introduced themselves. Some were from the Olsson side and the Andersons', and it would be a living nightmare to try and remember all their names.

"Grams! Grandpa!" Violet went running to her grandparents when she spotted them. Eric scooped her up and planted a kiss on her cheek.

Becca looked at her watch as she gave Sugar a hug. "Half hour late? Not bad for Sugar time." She was known for being late, more so when it was something she didn't want to do.

Sugar shrugged sheepishly. "Sorry. Emery wanted to talk about this deal and wouldn't let it go. I hope you didn't hold dinner for us."

Eric kissed her forehead and chuckled. "You're fine. Dinner won't start for two hours."

Placing her hands on her hips, Sugar gave Becca an accusatory look. "I do what I need to do to get things done," Becca said simply.

"Mom, look, there's Jackson! Can I go give him his thank you card?" Violet had worked diligently for days at her new table making an elaborate thank you card. Sugar had been so busy she hadn't been able to get to the hotel this week, and Violet insisted on giving it to him in person.

Sugar looked where Violet was pointing to see Jackson looking back at her. Their eyes locked across the crowded room, and the thought of that would have made her roll her eyes if he wasn't so damn handsome. In a light gray pin-striped suit and a crisp white shirt with no tie and the top button undone, he looked like he walked out of the page of a magazine. She didn't even mind the man bun or his full beard, which seemed to grow fuller the colder it got.

CR

Jackson saw her the minute she walked into the room. Her hair was partially up with wispy little pieces falling around her face and long beachy waves nearly reaching her waist in the back. The blue dress fit her like a glove, reaching just above her knee. The top above the bodice and sleeves were a delicate blue lace, and even from his vantage point, Jackson could see it accentuated her eyes.

All the thoughts about staying away from her flew right out of his mind in an instant. He tore his eyes from her as little Violet approached him. She looked cute as a button in her violet covered dress.

"Hi Jackson! I made this for you!" Violet said as she handed him a card. Jackson squatted down to her level and took it from her hands. The paper had little drawings all over it and said "THANK YOU" in bold letters that were obviously written by her.

When he opened it up, it had "I," and big red heart, and "U." Little hearts had been cut out and pasted all over it. He stared at it for a beat while he got control of his emotions. Jackson couldn't remember the last time he cried, but here he was about to open the flood gates in a room full of people over a card a little girl made him.

"This is the most beautiful thing anyone has ever given me," Jackson finally said. "Thank you, Violet." She launched herself at him and he gave her a good squeeze while kissing the top of her head.

☙

Finally alone, Sugar looked around the big family room. Violet was playing with all the other children, and Sugar needed a moment of silence. The house was busting with people, and they all wanted to talk to her about the café or the television show. She took out her phone and set an alarm for dinner, just in case she completely zoned out.

This wasn't a normal family room, not like any she had ever seen. Sugar didn't grow up in poverty or anything, but the sheer amount of wealth running through this family was obvious by this house. It was easy to forget the legacy that ran through her veins when most of the time Alec, Eric, and Becca came to her. Sugar's apartment must seem like a closet to Alec and Eric.

She might have envisioned something like this when she was young. The only thing Becca ever told her about her father was that he was a good man who couldn't be with them. She stuck to this until Sugar was seventeen when she revealed some of the truth. Being a creative child, Sugar would imagine her dad was some prince trapped by an evil force and one day he'd come back to them.

Yes, this kind of room was what she imagined. With the big billiard table and expensive leather furniture with rich, plush rugs and portraits on the walls, she could see her father here pining away for Becca and his little girl while some mystical force kept him away.

Of course as she grew older, Sugar knew this fantasy couldn't be the case, and she pushed and pushed until Becca told her the truth; well she told her part of the truth.

"Sugar, do you know how worried I was?" Becca demanded as her daughter came stumbling home at three a.m.

"I'm so sorry, Mom. My phone died, and we were working on the website, and I just fell asleep," Sugar said as she plopped down on the happy yellow couch in their living room. "I promise it won't happen again." It was partially true. She left out the part about sobering up before coming home.

Becca pulled her robe closed and sat down next to her daughter, grateful she was okay. "Sugar, I'm not stupid. I smelled the beer as soon as you walked in the door." She knew this was normal teenage rebellion, but she also knew that kids with ADHD faced bigger challenges and skewed toward risky behavior. Sugar may not need medicine anymore, but the symptoms would always be a part of her life.

Sugar laid back on the couch. "I didn't lie. My phone did die, and we were working."

"But you left the drinking part out. How did you get home?" Becca was about to her wits' end. Sugar always told her everything. When Sugar had sex with Josh for the first time, she came right home and told her. Becca almost wished she'd kept that to herself. It seemed like her kid was going off the rails, and she didn't know how to stop it.

"Emery. She was fine, Mother, she wasn't drinking." She wasn't. Emery was working away while Sugar and Josh partied.

"And was Emery's phone dead? Josh's?" Becca pushed.

"I don't know, I didn't ask." Sugar's head was starting to pound, and she really didn't want to deal with the third degree right now.

"I can't live like this, Sugar, and this behavior is going to stop. You're grounded for two weeks." Sugar started to protest so Becca raised her finger. "You want to make it a month?"

Sugar crossed her arms over her chest. "That's fine. It's Father's Day next weekend, so Josh and Emery can't do anything anyway."

Father's Day, that explains it. As Sugar grew older, they always had problems around this time of year. Sugar was a good kid. She excelled in culinary school and had a thriving business. Any kid in her position could tell their parents to get bent if they grounded them, but Becca knew Sugar would never do that. Deep down she was such a good kid.

"No phone, no internet, unless for school or work. No nothing. For two weeks you are stuck with me," Becca said.

"So you got nothing about the Father's Day comment?" Sugar asked.

"Sugar, we've been through this . . ." Becca started to say.

"No, Mom, no we haven't. I know nothing about my family

history except your mom was abusive, your father died, and my father can't be with us but would if he could. It's like we were dropped off here from another planet."

"Sweetheart, now is not the time," Becca said.

"It's never time." Sugar jumped up off the couch and stared her mother down. "When? When will it be time? Do you know what it's like not knowing anything about your past?"

"Sug, sit down." She didn't know if it was because she was tired or she realized how incredibly unfair it was to keep her daughter in the dark any longer, but she knew it was time to tell her the truth.

Sugar sat back down, feeling her heart beat in her chest.

"I've told you how I left my home because my own mother was abusive," she said as she took Sugar's hand as she nodded. "Your father, well I've loved him most of my life, since I was eight years old. We were best friends, and then more when we got older, like Josh and yourself."

Becca got a faraway look in her eyes as she continued. "We bonded at first because he had an abusive parent too, his father. He was a violent, cruel man. Three families owned a big business in our town, and your father's family was one of them. When we got older, his father decided that two of the families needed to be joined so his family kept control. He forced your father to marry one of the daughters from one of the other families."

Sugar tried to make sense of her mother's evasive confession. Her mom never said proper names when talking about the past, probably because she knew Sugar would be googling in a heartbeat.

"So he was married when you got pregnant with me?" Sugar asked quietly.

"Yes, he was, but it wasn't a real marriage."

Sugar snorted and started to say something about how all

married men said things like that, but the look on her mother's
face stopped her. Her poor mom believed it.

"When my father died, I went back home and had a horrible
fight with your grandmother. I decided that I wouldn't let my-
self go through her abuse anymore and was leaving when I ran
into your father."

"So he took advantage of you when you were grieving your
dad?" Sugar asked. Her heart broke into a million pieces as all
fantasies she had about her father were crushed.

"It wasn't like that, Sug. Like I said, we never stopped loving
each other, and your dad is a good man. I'll be grateful for that
until the day I die because it gave me you."

Sugar felt so bad for her mother. She was taken advantage
of at her own father's funeral and got saddled with a defective
kid like her. Sugar knew her mom had gone through hell and
back when Sugar was younger. All the problems at school, all the
doctors, all her issues; Sugar needed to start being better because
her mom had been through enough.

"So they have a lot of money?" Sugar asked.

"Well, yes, it's a very big business that supports the whole town."

"I've heard enough." If her father was the type of man that
would marry to stay wealthy, she didn't want to know anymore.

"Are you alright, Sugar?" Becca asked with concern.

"Are you alright, Sugar?" a voice boomed behind her.
Sugar was standing in front of a portrait of a woman that
looked so much like herself, she almost wondered if she
had posed for it and forgot.

"Yeah, I'm good. I just needed some quiet," Sugar said
as she turned to look at Eric.

"That," he said pointing at the picture, "is your Great
Grandmother Ingrid." He walked over and stood next to
Sugar. "My dad, your grandfather, loved her so much. I

know your mom was always afraid of what he might do if he knew about you, but one look at you and it would have been over. He would have given you the world."

Sugar didn't know how to feel about that. Since coming back to this town all those weeks ago, she learned so much. Her grandfather did whatever it took to protect the family business. Paul Anderson, one of the partners, had a quickie marriage that threatened the business when he was young, and during the divorce proceedings, she had driven off the side of the mountain. Most thought her grandfather had something to do with it, but it couldn't be proven.

He had reminded Eric of this when he told him he was going to marry Allison Olsson, and that something like failed brakes could easily happen to Becca. How would Sugar have turned out if raised like the golden child of a vast family fortune? How would she have turned out if she didn't have to go through all the struggles she went through over the course of her life?

She needed to give her mom an extra big hug the next time she saw her.

Emery was right. Sugar did have issues with the rich. Even though she worked incredibly hard and had done it all herself, Sugar still didn't want to count herself in their ranks. Her eyes were opened.

Another portrait had three men with their arms casually draped on each other's shoulders. It looked like it was taken in the 1940s and the men all wore wide smiles.

"They are the men that started all of this," Eric said as he gestured around the room.

He walked to the next portrait, with three different men. "There's my father, Paul, and Allison's father."

Sugar knew Paul Anderson without her father pointing him out. His younger self bared a striking resemblance to his son. This picture seemed much more formal, and the three men stood apart from each other. "They weren't close? Like their dads were?" Sugar asked.

"Heavens no. Paul and your grandfather despised each other. Allison's father swung back and forth between them, picking and choosing which side to be on."

"That's why your dad was worried."

Eric sighed. "Pretty much. According to Paul, my father wasn't always terrible. He thinks something happened to him when he was a pre-teen, that everything about him changed. We'll never know."

"We all have our own bullshit," Sugar said as she looked at the next picture. There was usually a reason why people were terrible. Eric didn't have to point out that this picture was her grandmother. Eric was a perfect hybrid of his parents.

"Yes, we do. Madison and Alec don't know just how bad their grandfather was," Eric said carefully. "They know he wasn't the best person in the world, but they think I married their mother because I was afraid of him, and they don't know about Paul's first wife. I figured that is on a need-to-know basis."

"I get that. They won't hear it from me."

"Thank you." He went back to the picture of his father. "He was a decent grandfather. After the marriage he calmed down quite a bit. It would be easier if I could just hate him, but I guess no matter what they do, we still love the people who raised us."

"I hated you," Sugar admitted. "I hated you for so long."

"I know. I can't say I'd blame you," Eric said. He knew

the whole story. "I can't imagine being in Becca's shoes and having to explain everything to my child."

"Me either. I can't imagine being in your shoes either. It's a girl, and she's twenty-five," Sugar joked.

"When did you know that you loved Violet?" Eric asked, tilting his head slightly to the side.

"What? The minute I saw her, of course."

"I was the same with Madison and Alec, and I can tell you from experience, it doesn't matter if they are one minute old or twenty-five, the feeling is the same the first time you lay eyes on your child."

Sugar was saved from the lump that developed in her throat when her phone's alarm went off. "Dinner," she said. "We better go or my mom is going to kill us."

Chapter 7

EVEN THOUGH STIFF AND FORMAL, dinner was delicious. Sugar felt weird being served but quickly forgot about it when she saw how happy her daughter was. Violet was having a blast with her newfound family, and even if it wasn't what Sugar envisioned a family holiday was as a child, she was glad her child could experience a big, traditional Thanksgiving.

"It just highlighted how women are treated," Allison, Eric's ex-wife was saying. Just the core family was left, and they all retired to the family room with the portraits.

Sugar tried to pay attention, but she was so tired of all this #metoo talk. The baking show had made a small ripple in American culture, and the judge's not so subtle flirting and the way that ass Bob acted sparked several hashtags that trended on Twitter.

She rarely posted for herself, usually Emery did all that, but when Sugar realized the frenzy, she did a post of her own. She was still stinging from Jasmine's comments about her.

#metoo doesn't stand a chance until we as women start supporting each other and stop being so catty. #youtoo.

Sugar truly believed in the #metoo movement but really did believe it would never succeed until women started treating each other with respect. God knows she had her problems over the years, but the simple truth was women had hurt her much more than the men ever did.

That post created another tidal wave on social media. Some agreed, some said she was victim blaming, and a new hashtag started trending: #tallbeautifulwhitegirlproblems.

Figuring Emery would be pissed, Sugar was surprised when Emery was absolutely thrilled. "No publicity is bad publicity," she had said.

Deep down she knew Jasmine didn't mean the couple of comments she made about her, but she didn't need to say them to begin with. The producers were doing a job—to create a character. They switched tact with Sugar after they realized she wasn't going to be the resident ditz and tried to get her to talk about Josh and the hardships of financially supporting her daughter all alone.

Thankfully she didn't fall for that, because who Becca was had come out too. #tallbeautifulwhitegirlproblems turned into #richtallbeautifulwhitegirlproblems. It would have been so much worse if she would have said things like, "I need to win to help support my little girl because there is only me," like they had asked her to say over and over.

"Hunter's comments always circled around to your looks instead of your talent," Mary, Allison's wife, was saying.

Hunter was really taking a beating on social media for his behavior. Sugar knew the judges were also playing a part. For being reality television, it sure was fake.

"He had zero interest in me," Sugar said as she looked around for Violet, wanting to escape. "Like none. He was playing a part, and even joked about it behind the scenes." Hunter's image was all about being a bad boy heartbreaker.

"I bet he regrets that now," Allison said.

"Possibly." Even though the situation was popular on Twitter for a few days, that didn't mean the population at large was all caught up in it. Sugar wouldn't have known about it if she wasn't involved. Despite making a good living on social media, she barely ever used it for personal reasons. Social media reminded her of high school run amok. For the first time she wondered if this would hurt his career.

She spotted Violet who was chatting with Madison. Sugar had successfully managed to stay away from her half-sister all day and was still wary about her daughter spending time with the woman.

Sugar had problems with people like Madison her whole life. From the seventh graders who relished the false story about her showing her boobs to a boy, to the girls who did the unthinkable during her freshman year, she had dealt with it all.

Eric said Madison had changed, but it was hard to believe when the first time she talked to the woman, Madison's first instinct was to try and make Sugar feel small. She was his kid, so Eric was biased.

Excusing herself to check on Violet, Sugar was relieved when her little girl floated over to Jessica, her friend from school. She needed to be around kids more. Being an only child, Violet had spent most of her young years in the company of adults.

"Are you two having fun?" Sugar asked. They really needed to leave soon. The café was all decorated for Christmas as they had done it that morning, but tomorrow would be another crazy day and Sugar wanted to get some sleep for once.

Both girls nodded in unison. "Mom, can we play Minecraft? Please?"

"Just for a little bit. We have to get going soon, okay?"

Violet pouted but shook her head yes. The two little girls giggled and sat together in one of the big leather chairs while Sugar pulled up the app on the tablet. Seeing that everyone was busy mingling, Sugar saw her chance to escape for a moment.

Stealthily leaving the room, Sugar walked down the long hallway to a sitting room with large windows facing the mountains. The moon shined bright, and the view was spectacular. Distracted by the beautiful view, Sugar didn't notice the other person she'd avoided all day.

Jackson.

He was sitting on the couch enjoying the view and had removed his suit jacket. His long legs stretched before him. "Did you need to escape the madness too?" he asked.

It was too late to turn back now, so she tried to ignore the leap in her stomach and the jump in her pulse rate. "Something like that," Sugar said. He patted the space on the couch next to him, so she reluctantly joined him.

"This must be very different to how you're used to celebrating Thanksgiving."

Sugar laughed. *One dimple.* "You have no idea. Right now, we'd be in sweatpants miserably waiting for the food coma to kick in."

"When I was young, we would go to my mother's side

for holidays sometimes. They were chaotic and informal. I preferred that to this grandeur. It can be overwhelming, and I grew up with it."

Sugar pointed to the mountain view. "You also got to grow up with this. I mean, the ocean is amazing, but this view, it's just inspiring."

"And with great people. It's got to be nice for you to spend the holidays with a big family."

"For the most part," Sugar said.

Jackson noticed how Sugar avoided Madison like the plague. "Madison?" he asked.

"Madison and I have a relationship that's just the way I want it. Distant and cold."

"She's not that bad," he said. Sugar looked at him incredulously and he bumped her shoulder with his. Both of them tried to ignore the jolt of electricity that came from the contact.

"Really, she's not. She has her issues, like anyone else, but for the most part she's a decent person."

"I bet Holly from the flower shop would disagree, and considering how my first meeting with her went down, I would too."

Jackson tucked one of his long legs underneath him and turned to face Sugar. "Ah, Holly. I bet an eight-year-old Madison would say that Holly was the one that was terrible. I have no excuses for how Madison treated her in high school, but when they were younger, Madison was dished her fair share of bullshit from Holly."

Sugar's brow furrowed. "That doesn't seem like the Holly I know."

Jackson shrugged. "She grew up. Like I said, there is no excuse for how Madison treated her in high school, but there's a reason why Holly was her target. I remember Madison crying her eyes out at her eighth birthday party because Holly told her no one liked her and people only came because of The Lodge. Those two have a long history of trying to one up each other. Madison just won."

"No one wins in that situation," Sugar pointed out.

"Absolutely not, but I thought you could use some perspective on the situation."

"What are you? The Larssons' cheerleader?"

"Rah, rah?" Jackson shook fake pom-poms in the air as Sugar laughed. *Two dimples.*

"Anyway, what about you? Any bullies lurking in your past?" Sugar asked. She didn't want to talk about Madison anymore, and she certainly didn't want to feel sorry for her.

"I was always twice as big as the other kids, so no, I never worried about that."

Sugar leaned back into the couch, relaxing for the first time all day. "And your parents owned half the town," she pointed out.

Jackson settled in too, their shoulders touching slightly. "Technically they only own a third," he joked. "My gramps and dad were never into all of the money or status like their counterparts were. If I ever acted like I was better than anyone else, my dad would have kicked my ass."

"I love your dad. You can tell he could give a shit what people think."

Somehow their position had changed and Sugar was resting comfortably in the nook of his arm. He smelled like a fresh winter day but spicy and warm at the same time. She felt safe, which seemed like a ridiculous thing to think. It was still nice, and he radiated heat, which her California blood appreciated.

"For sure. I think that's why they shipped me off in the summer to my grandparents in the south. It's hard not to be humble when you are being used as a farm-hand." He didn't know how it happened, but his arm was casually around Sugar's shoulders, and she was comfortably resting in the nook. He didn't know if it was because of her cooking or perfume, but she smelled as sweet as her name.

"And Alec went with you?"

Jackson was absentmindedly trailing his fingers up and down her upper arm, causing small tingles to run through her body.

"Yep. There was always a fight with Eric's dad over it, but he stood his ground. Eric knew it was important for us to see a different way of life, and John Larsson thought Alec should be learning the business, not off somewhere farming."

"I worry about Violet living here, if I decide to stay," Sugar admitted. "I don't want her to grow up being the crowned princess of the town."

"What do you mean, if you decide to stay? You aren't going anywhere," he said confidently.

Sugar slapped his hard chest as he let out a low, sexy laugh in the back of his throat. "How do you know that?"

"Because we both know how precious life is and how it can be over in an instant. It's too damn short, and we don't want to waste precious time being away from those we love. That's why I'm here, and that's why you'll stay."

"I don't see my mom leaving here anytime soon." He

was right. Deep down Sugar was still the four-year-old clinging to her mother's legs, not wanting to leave her. She may be fiercely independent, but another part of her would always need her mama.

"No, I suppose not. And Violet? You have zero worries when it comes to her."

"Worry is part of the job when you become a parent," Sugar said.

"Did you tell her to make me a thank you card?" Jackson questioned. Sugar shook her head no. "See, that's what I mean. She is kind and thoughtful because that's what you've taught her to be. Hell, I almost teared up in a room full of people when she gave me that card. It was so sweet and sincere."

Sugar sat up so she could look at him directly. "You did not."

Jackson chuckled. "Scout's honor," he said as he held up two fingers. "It's going on my refrigerator next to her other picture."

Sugar's face softened and she positively melted. "Her picture is on your refrigerator?"

"Of course. It makes me smile every morning." Jackson was expecting another dimple but realized he was going to get something much better as she started to lean in toward him.

"Sugar, are you back here?" Becca called out as she entered the room. She hoped she hid the smile on her face when Jackson and Sugar jumped apart, looking like two guilty teenagers caught making out.

"Yeah, what's up, Mom? Is Violet okay?" Sugar and Jackson both stood up quickly, standing at attention.

"She's fine, sweetheart. Eric wants everyone to gather

together for a minute," Becca said hiding her knowing smile.

Jesus, I almost kissed him again, Sugar thought as they walked back to the main family room. She shouldn't be alone with him.

The temptation would be great as her mind seemed to quiet around him. Even though she didn't take medication anymore, her mind still worked differently than most people's minds, and it could be exhausting. When you found something that contained your focus, it was exhilarating, relaxing, and addictive all at the same time.

Not guaranteed to last, hyper focus could lead to hurt feelings. She learned that lesson the hard way with Josh.

Becca walked over to Eric as he motioned for everyone to gather around. He put both arms around Becca and kissed her cheek.

"I know everyone is tired. We need to create our own family holiday that isn't around the normal ones." Most of the people in the room spent their morning getting ready for Christmas and would likely be finishing after the family Thanksgiving was over. In their line of business, holidays were exhausting.

"I'm so happy that despite how tired we are, we can come together with the people we love. We have more to be thankful for this year than ever," he said as he looked at Sugar and Violet, "and since we are all together, Becks and I wanted to make a little announcement. We're getting married on Christmas Day."

The room erupted in cheers as everybody crowded around the couple to offer congratulations. Sugar stood rooted to her spot, truly shocked.

"Emery wants to talk to you. Your mom had me video

chat her so she could see their announcement," Alec said as he handed her his phone and headed over to congratulate the newly engaged couple.

"Sugar!" Emery said as she snapped her fingers a few times. "Now is not the time to freak out. Take me to your mother so I can congratulate her, and be nice!"

"They've only been together a few weeks," Sugar said to the screen.

"Please don't lead with that when you congratulate them."

Sugar looked over at her mom who was smiling widely as she hugged Alec. She looked so damn happy. Emery was saying something about how could Sugar be so smart and so clueless at the same time, but she wasn't paying attention. She needed to get it together.

She handed the phone to Becca as Emery started gushing. Eric hugged her as she said congratulations, and he gave her his signature kiss on her forehead.

"Oh, Sug, I was going to tell you, but we decided it should be a surprise," Becca said as she hugged her daughter tightly.

"Congratulations, I'm happy for you," Sugar said with a smile.

"Do I get to be the flower girl, Grams?" Violet asked as she clung to Becca's legs.

Becca laughed and scooped her up. "Of course! There is no one better for the job."

After the fanfare died down, Sugar got Violet dressed to go into the cold and back home. Even though it was only a little after her bedtime, Violet was exhausted and it showed.

"But we need to get a tree tomorrow," Violet whined.

They had decorated the café that morning and used the tree and decorations Sugar ordered online and bought around town. Sugar promised Violet they could get a real tree for the apartment that weekend.

"Violet, tomorrow is a very busy day. Everyone goes shopping for Christmas tomorrow, so we have to work at the café. I told you we'll go Saturday and get one." She rapidly wrapped her scarf around her neck and zipped up her coat because she knew they were headed for meltdown territory. Tantrums were few and far between now that she was older, but when she was tired, they could still rear their ugly head.

The tears were about to fall when she heard Jackson's voice behind her. "Did I hear someone say they need a tree?"

"I need a tree so Santa will come," Violet said, her little bottom lip quivering.

"Well I happen to know a place that takes you into the woods on a horse and sleigh to pick out your tree," Jackson said.

Violet loved horses. Back when they stayed at Jackson's hotel, she told him they should have some, and Sugar was surprised he remembered.

"Really?" Violet asked, her tears temporarily forgotten.

"Really. The only thing is, I can't take you there until Saturday because I have to work tomorrow. Do you think you could wait?"

"Oh yes, I can wait! Mommy and I have to work at the café tomorrow anyway!"

So much for staying away from him, Sugar thought. Still grateful for his quick thinking and the fact Violet forgot to call her plain Mom, she kissed his cheek and squeezed his arm. "Thank you, Jackson, that's very kind of you."

He smiled at the two of them. "It's my pleasure."

CR

Madison was back in her opulent apartment at The Lodge making a list of the things she needed to do tomorrow. Things at The Lodge were in full swing for the holidays, which meant work, work, and more work.

She certainly didn't have time to take Sugar and Violet to get a tree. Madison was leaving the main house when she heard Jackson's offer and saw Sugar's intimate response. Perhaps the rumor mill was right this time.

Madison's friends gave her a play by play via text since Sugar had moved there. Allegedly, Jackson made Violet some elaborate table or something, and according to them, it must have been because he wanted in Sugar's pants.

That was utterly ridiculous. Jackson never dated women with children. She wasn't sure if he even liked children. It shouldn't bother her since she had no interest in him that way, but she knew her catty friends told her all this with a gleam in their eye, thinking it would make her jealous.

No, she gave up on having a thing with Jackson long ago. She was more like a little sister to him, and if she was honest, he was nowhere near her type either. Her grandfather always talked about the two of them getting married and finally combining all three families, and for a long time she dreamt of that. It did make sense, but look at her parents. Two people not in love didn't make for a good marriage.

She supposed if Sugar and Jackson got married, it would accomplish the same goal, but that would be a disaster. Her new half-sister didn't like her, not that she could blame her. Madison's behavior had been less than stellar the first time they met, and she went and made it worse by lying to Eric about it.

If Alec wouldn't have called her on it and blackmailed her into telling the truth, who knows what would have happened. Maybe Sugar wouldn't even be here and her mother wouldn't be marrying Eric. Madison knew her father, and she knew he would be giving Sugar her share of The Lodge. Her dad was a good man and did the right thing.

But was it the right thing? Sugar never worked a day here. Sure, some could say her celebrity caused the off-shoot hotel to be successful, but Madison hardly thought of that as a positive. She patiently waited for it to fail so they could go back to what they were—a luxury hotel. That wasn't going to happen now, and Jackson was already talking about expanding.

If Sugar had a share in the trust, she would vote for what Jackson wanted of course. Alec defaulted to what Jackson wanted because he knew it would upset her, so she would just be screwed.

She could pull out a few of her old shenanigans, except that wouldn't work. They had called her on her behavior immediately and closed ranks with her previous attempt at sabotage, and even though friendly to her, Becca made it perfectly clear—they had dealt like with people like her in the past, and if she pulled any crap like that again, she would lose.

People might think that people like her were scary,

but Madison knew nothing was scarier than a genuinely nice person who gets angry.

In the past Madison could always count on her father having her back, but now she wasn't so sure. She should have known better, but she swore her father treated her differently since he found out he had a shiny new daughter.

Deep down she knew this wasn't true, but a small part of her still believed it.

She laid back on her big elegant canopy bed. She loved this bed. With its expensive sheets and hand embroidered duvet, it made her feel special, like she was royalty. Opening up her laptop, she logged into Alec's Facebook account. He may be good at many things, but cyber security was not one of them. She could always guess his passwords.

Sugar didn't seem to have any personal social media accounts, but Emery did. She couldn't contain the small smile when she saw the litany of messages Emery had fired off at Alec. Not daring to open them, she could tell by the first line she read on each of them that she was really putting Alec through his paces.

Emery's personal Facebook was private, but since her idiot brother couldn't seem to form a password that didn't involve one of their childhood pets, Madison had full access. Emery was smart. She graduated with honors from Stanford and was in a sorority.

The picture of her with her parents cleared up a bit about Emery's ambiguous ancestry. Her mother was a light-skinned African American, and her tall, blonde-haired father would have fit in this town perfectly.

Emery wasn't kidding when she bragged about her

parents' success. A side trip to Google showed her that the Coopers were a power couple in the entertainment industry and had some very high-profile clients.

Madison thought back to when she first met Sugar and Emery. She knew she was rude to them, pointing out that Becca and Sugar shouldn't get their hopes up about receiving any of the fruits from The Lodge. Just because she was rude didn't make the sting any less when Emery replied, *"You know, this place would probably be great for some of my parents' clients. I don't know if I could recommend it though, if this is how the help acts, no matter how nice your father is."*

Oh, how she wished she wouldn't have started the relationship the way she did. Madison didn't have a clue that Becca Jones was Marie Jones, the best-selling author. She also didn't know anything about Emery's parents. It was pure instinct that made her be rude to them. People had tried to get a little piece of the Larsson pie since she was a kid. She was just being protective.

Scrolling through her pictures she wondered not for the first time how Emery maintained a friendship with Sugar for so long. Even though she didn't know either woman well, they seemed as different as night and day. Under different circumstances, she could see herself being friends with Emery. They were both driven and focused.

Madison landed on a #TBT picture labeled "Sugar, Josh, and me at the Sugar Jones LLC celebration."

She checked the date on the picture and figured they were about eighteen years old when it was taken. Tilting her head to the side, she checked out Josh, Violet's father. *He was way beneath her*, she thought unkindly.

He was attractive, in a geeky kind of way, but she pictured Sugar with someone more like herself—annoyingly good looking. If she saw the two of them together, she would assume he was her friend, and she bet most people did.

Josh did have an infectious smile and what appeared to be pretty blue eyes behind his glasses. He was just a smidge taller than Sugar and appeared to be thin. If this was Sugar's type, Jackson didn't stand a chance in hell.

Landing on a picture of Emery and Sugar at the beach with a blurred-out Violet in the background, she almost threw up in her mouth a little. You couldn't even tell Sugar gave birth. Of course her body would remain perfection. What Madison wouldn't do to have a body like that.

She loved fashion, but since she was so short, everything she bought had to be tailored. Sugar could probably buy straight from the runway and wear anything she wanted, but from what she saw in person and these pictures, she not only wore yoga pants most of the time, but she usually didn't even match.

Plotting against these two wasn't a smart idea, and one thing Madison wasn't was stupid. That didn't mean she couldn't have a little fun.

Picking up her cell phone she called Carrie, a frenemy who loved to gossip.

She asked her how her Thanksgiving was and listened impatiently as she droned on and on about it, trying to impress Madison.

"Ours was perfect as usual," Madison said. "I am a little worried about my half-sister though."

"Really? Why would you be worried about her?" Carrie asked with fake sincerity.

"Oh, I'm just starting to wonder if maybe Jackson is putting the moves on her. You promise you won't say anything to anyone?" Madison asked.

"Of course not!" Carrie said. "You can trust me."

Madison wouldn't trust Carrie any farther than she could throw her. "Well, Sugar is new in town. She probably has no idea about Jackson's reputation. It's complicated with our family and business connections, so I can't say anything, but they disappeared together for part of the day. People had to actually search for them. I just hope the poor thing knows Jackson doesn't get serious."

She smiled as she hung up the phone. That would get people talking, and they'd go straight to Sugar and tell her what a player Jackson was.

Chapter 8

"HOW MUCH LONGER, MOM?" Violet, drawing at her beautiful little table in the café kitchen, had asked her this every five minutes for the last hour.

"Five minutes less than the last time you asked," Sugar said. So excited to go get a real tree with real horses and of course, Jackson, Violet pursed her lips and blew out an impatient, exaggerated breath.

They always had a teeny tiny tree in their small apartment in San Diego, the sad little kind that sat on a table because it was too small to sit on the floor. The big tree was always at Becca's beach house, where they would spend the night on Christmas Eve and wait for Santa. Even though she had created a successful business and raised a child by herself for four years, Sugar had never felt more like an adult than today.

She wanted to go to the hotel to meet Jackson, but he insisted on picking them up since the weather was calling for snow that afternoon. Sugar didn't like to drive under perfect conditions, so while she appreciated the gesture, she wondered how much him picking them up here would get tongues wagging around town.

Emery called her on Friday insisting to know the details of their disappearance on Thanksgiving. Even though she was all the way in San Diego, she had heard about their reentrance into the room before Eric and her mom's announcement. Several "concerned" people wanted to make sure Sugar was aware of Jackson's reputation with women, and they told Emery all about it.

One more day and Emery would be back in town, much to Sugar's relief. She wondered not for the first time if she'd be able to talk her into moving here. Emery really thrived here. It may not be a big city, but Emery had made a real difference in this town, in these people's lives. In a month's time, she'd put this town on the map.

Her current boyfriend, Todd, was not happy with all the travel, and Emery was not happy with how he was acting. He traveled for his job all the time and she understood, but he didn't give her the same consideration. Sugar knew Emery wasn't completely invested in him, and his recent behavior should be the final nail in that relationship coffin.

The two friends had correctly deduced that Madison must be behind the slew of new rumors. Who at the family Thanksgiving would start gossip like that? All signs pointed to Madison, but they couldn't figure out why. Wanting to deal with it herself, Sugar hadn't said anything to her mom or Eric yet, but this bullshit would get old fast if she was going to live here.

Besides, Madison would deny it. Sugar was well aware how it would go down. Madison would point out that they had a house full of people and pretend to be hurt that she was being blamed. Becca would believe Sugar, and Eric would stick up for Madison, causing a rift.

She still didn't know how she felt about their impending marriage, but Sugar had never seen her Mom so happy. Becca had always put Sugar first, so Sugar would try and put Becca first this time. She could deal with a few small-town whispers over nothing if it meant her mom had a chance at real happiness.

Sugar's alarm went off on her phone. It was time to get ready.

✷

It was a perfect winter day for going out into the woods and picking out a Christmas tree. Big fat flakes of snow were falling all around them as the Clydesdale horses pulled their sleigh through the tree farm, happy bells jingling. Jackson jumped through hoops and wheeled and dealed to make this happen, but seeing the magic and wonder on Violet's face made it all worth it.

Normally this sleigh was used for late-night sleigh rides at The Lodge, not for getting trees. Thankfully the fresh blanket of snow put the farmer's fears at ease that it would damage his land. When the man found out Jackson wanted to do this for Violet and Sugar, it swayed the decision to let him do it.

This town wasn't about to look a gift horse in the mouth, and Sugar's popularity and Emery's hard work had the whole town jumping. There hadn't been this much growth and opportunity since they first started building the town all those decades ago.

He assumed that's why several people reminded him these last couple days that Sugar was a widow and had a kid, like he didn't know that already. Derrick, the night manager at the hotel, told him people were talking about how Sugar and Jackson had to be found on Thanksgiving, and he assumed people were afraid he would break their new valuable citizen's heart.

Madison. It had to be Madison who said something. Normally he was saved from Madison's schemes and gossip, and he didn't appreciate being inducted into the fold of hapless victims, especially since he always stood up for her.

She had given up on the two of them having anything more than a friendship years ago, so he didn't understand why she was doing this. Maybe Alec was right about Madison. She was just an asshole. He'd been so busy that he hadn't been able to talk to her yet, but he planned on doing just that before things got out of hand.

Violet sat between the two of them with Thor looking up at her with adoration from his place by their feet.

Looking at Sugar pointing out different sights to Violet as they rode along, he wondered if anyone had said anything to her. Of course they had; nothing stayed silent in this town, especially if someone from The Lodge's families was involved. She didn't seem to be acting any different than normal, so maybe he was fretting over nothing.

When did I start fretting? Jackson thought.

The sleigh slowed to a stop. They were in a lovely spot full of Colorado blue spruce trees. Usually the trees were harvested and sent to stores to be sold, but there were still plenty left for them to choose. Jackson thanked the driver and the farmer as he helped Violet and Sugar down from the sleigh. Grabbing an axe, he joined the excited little girl and her mother as they looked around in wonder.

Violet ran up to a majestic blue spruce followed closely by Thor. Standing at least thirty feet tall, Jackson smiled. "How about this one, Mommy?"

Sugar smiled and shook her head at Jackson. He had stopped counting dimples as there had already been so many. He learned one thing today. Violet being happy equaled Sugar being happy. "How is that going to fit in our apartment, monkey?" Sugar asked.

"We probably shouldn't pick one that is taller than me," Jackson said to Violet as he crouched down to her level. "The bigger ones have been here a long time. Probably a lot of birds live here, and we don't want to take away their homes."

"Okay!" Violet moved on, looking at some of the smaller trees.

"What do you think our chances are that she'll like a four-footer?" Jackson asked.

"Slim to none," Sugar said. The snow was falling all around her and a few hefty flakes were on her eyelashes. She had on this ridiculous black coat that made her look three sizes bigger than she really was, and it just charmed Jackson all the more.

Violet, in her more fashionable pink snow suit, called out to Jackson. "Can you please come stand by this one?" Doing as he was told, he seriously stood next to the tree. It was a great tree, round and full and a few inches shorter than Jackson.

"I think you found it," Sugar said as she stood next to her little girl. Agreeing that it was the perfect tree, Jackson started preparing the spruce to cut it down.

"First, let's make sure no birds live here," Jackson said as he looked over the tree and gave it a good shake.

Squatting down he started to remove branches from the bottom. He asked the girls to stand back as he choked up on his axe handle.

"Wouldn't that be easier with a chain saw?" Sugar asked.

"This'll do the job just fine," Jackson answered.

"I don't like chain saws. They are scary," Violet said seriously. "I don't like loud noise."

"I don't either," Jackson said seriously. Sugar tilted her head to the side and looked at him quizzically.

☙

After making quick work of cutting down the tree and the sleigh ride back to their car, they brought the tree back to Sugar's apartment. Jackson and Violet were setting up the tree in a big bucket of water, and Smidge and Branch were acting like Disneyland had come to their new home. Not only was there a new tree, but their old friend Thor had joined the fold.

Jackson was pouring a concoction of sugar water and maple syrup into the bucket. "The tree's sleeping and this will wake it up. You know how we have blood in our veins? The tree has sugar in its veins, and this will make it not drop as many needles. You have to make sure it always has water, or it'll go to sleep again and all the needles will fall off."

"I will Jackson, I promise!"

He was so good with her. Currently in the kitchen making dinner, Sugar was amazed at how he seemed to instinctively cut off any of the normal four-year-old tantrums. Since it was Violet's day, Sugar was making her eternal favorite mac-n-cheese, the only food item she didn't need to be reminded to eat.

"Are you sure we can't decorate it now?" Violet asked hopefully.

"Sorry, you have to wait another day. The branches are still cold, so if you put the lights on them now, the branches would be stuck up in the air."

"That's okay! It looks perfect like this!"

Jackson squinted his eyes at her. "Would your hair look perfect if it always looked like this?" he asked as he picked her up and turned her upside down.

Violet erupted in giggles. "Noooooo, I would look silly, Jackson." He turned her right side up and plopped her on the floor, laughing.

He's a natural father, Sugar thought. Patient and kind, but firm, this all came so naturally to him. Sugar could tell he was enjoying himself just as much as her little girl. He wasn't one of those guys being nice to Violet because he was interested in Sugar. There had been a couple of guys like that in the past, and Jackson couldn't be more different than them if he tried.

She tried not to get all up in her own head over that stray thought. Jackson was being nice because he was her friend and he cared for Violet. There was no need to freak out over this.

One thing was for sure. He was nothing like who she thought he was that first night in Snow Valley when she rolled into town. She should know better than to judge a book by its cover with her own experiences, but it must be human nature to do so.

Sugar assumed he would be one of those arrogant guys on Instagram, all full of himself and conceited.

Since they met, he proved over and over he was nothing like that. Nice, kind, and humble described him better.

Remembering the rumors about him, at least there was one thing she got right that night. He liked the ladies and loved them often, lots of them. Even though people said he wasn't the kind of guy to get serious, they were quick to add that he wasn't the type to say whatever it took to hook up. It seemed he found like-minded women who were just wanting a good time.

Could she be like that? There was no doubt that physically she wanted him. Sugar hadn't exactly been a saint since Josh died, and she refused to feel ashamed for being a woman who sometimes needed physical contact. Over the years many had tried to make her feel that way, and she wasn't having it.

The problem was she liked him. Having a casual affair with someone you cared for was a recipe for disaster. They would be tied together for a long time. She wasn't sure if just liking him would turn into something more if they went there.

After dinner and a rousing couple of games of Chutes and Ladders, Violet was asleep, and he was still here. There would be no people interrupting them this time, and Sugar was nervous. How was it possible that she wished he would leave while hoping he would stay at the same time?

Softly pulling Violet's bedroom door halfway closed, she looked back at her sleeping daughter. The two kittens had taken their positions on each side of her as they did every night, and Thor laid at the end of the bed.

"You realize she's going to want a dog too now," Sugar said as she took her spot in her favorite chair, wrapping her favorite quilt around her shoulders. She almost sat next to him on the comfortable couch, but decided that would be a bad idea.

Jackson chuckled. "I guess this place wouldn't be big enough for a dog like Thor, and my guess is she'd want a big dog." He settled back in the couch, comfortably relaxed as he cradled his hot cocoa.

"This apartment is downright palatial compared to my place in San Diego," Sugar told him. "The whole apartment could probably fit in this living room."

"Do you miss it? San Diego?"

Sugar thought about this. Being so busy with the café and her newfound family, she really didn't have time to think about it. "I miss the warmth for sure, and all the activities that come with it. My mom keeps telling me my mountain blood will come in, but I'm not so sure."

"Moving to a new climate takes getting used to for sure," Jackson said. "When I first went to Afghanistan, I couldn't believe anywhere could be that hot."

"How long were you there?"

"About a year," Jackson said as his face clouded over and he shook it off, "but that was years ago. I'll take the changing of the seasons over always the same every time."

Sugar wanted to ask more but decided against it. She had heard Jackson went through some stuff over there, but if he wanted to tell her, he would. Remembering his comments about not liking loud noises, she felt a wave of compassion for him.

"The snow is beautiful," Sugar said, taking a sip of her own hot cocoa. "I suppose I'll appreciate it more when I have time to get out there and ski."

Jackson smiled. "I hear you. We've been so busy at the

hotel, I haven't hit the slopes much either. Ever since this television star moved to town, it's been downright crazy there," he teased.

Sugar rolled her big eyes and snorted. "I'm hardly a television star," she said. "By the time January rolls around, the general public will have forgotten all about it."

Leaning over and placing his elbows on his knees, Jackson looked at Sugar intently. "You really enjoy it though, don't you? The competition part of it?"

She thought about this. He was right—she did enjoy it. Sugar loved being a mom, the bakery, and the creative aspect of sugarjones.com, but while she was in the thick of the competition, she felt exhilarated.

"I suppose I did. I've gotten a few offers for other competition shows, but I've given our admin strict orders to shelve all emails about the TV show. I have too much going on here and will deal with all that after Christmas. Besides, the creep factor has went way up and I don't need that in my head now."

"Creep factor?" Jackson asked. His brow furrowed as he intently looked at Sugar.

She had said too much. Even back when the site only showed her hands, she would get creepy messages from people with hand fetishes. The internet and television opened you up to all kinds of people, and some of them weren't necessarily nice.

"Oh, you know, just some men who decide they want to marry me or whatever." She waved her hand in the air to dismiss it.

Jackson set his coffee cup down on the table. "Does Eric know about this? It sounds like it could be dangerous."

Truth be told, her mother and Eric knew nothing

about it. They were completely wrapped up in getting to know each other again.

Sugar also had the feeling that Eric wouldn't let her out of his sight if he knew some of the messages and emails she received. While he may not be a hardened man like his father, Eric had learned enough from him to get what he wanted, when he wanted it. Eric Larsson was not used to hearing the word no.

"Eric doesn't need to know about it," Sugar said as she watched Jackson's face fall in dismay. The blanket fell from her shoulders as she leaned forward toward him. "They're planning their wedding and are just as busy as everyone else. He's not going to know about it," she said pointedly.

"I don't think that's the right decision," Jackson said.

Sugar sighed. "Jackson, it's really not a big deal. Look at this place! It's as secure as Fort Knox. If someone were to actually break in, both the police and the security at The Lodge would be notified immediately."

Jackson crossed his muscled arms over his chest stubbornly. "And when you aren't here? What then?"

This situation was spiraling out of control. Sugar knew all of this came with the territory. Growing up in California, she spent her fair share of time around celebrities because of Emery's parents. More than likely, her admirers were harmless.

"My admin knows to alert us if someone seems dangerous."

"And just how exactly would she know that?" Jackson asked as he moved to the end of the couch, closer to Sugar.

"If someone seems obsessive, emailing or sending

messages over and over," Sugar said, breathing out an exasperated breath. "This is normal, Jackson. We know how to deal with it."

"It's not normal," he argued, crossing his arms across his chest once more. "If you insist on keeping this quiet, then I'll just have to keep an eye on you myself."

Sugar crossed her own arms across her chest. "You do realize I'm a grown woman, right? I'm perfectly capable of taking care of myself and my child."

"Did I say you weren't capable?" Jackson asked in a quiet voice, causing Sugar to look up. There was so much emotion in those words and written all over his face. She could tell he was really worried.

Sugar moved next to Jackson on the couch. "Jackson," she said, taking one of his hands in hers. "Every female on the planet gets creepy messages from men if they have any kind of social media account. I just reach more creeps."

"I'll start by walking Violet to school in the mornings," Jackson said, ignoring her statement.

Sugar let go of his hand and threw her own up in the air. "You are insufferable. Look, I appreciate that you want to look out for us," she said, "but doing something like that would really get people talking in town."

Jackson leaned toward Sugar, his face inches from hers. "I don't give a fuck what people in town say," he said with dead seriousness.

His aqua blue eyes seared into hers as she quickly inhaled. Feeling herself being drawn in like a moth to a flame, she somehow found the strength to lean back from him. Reigning in her wayward hormones and the foreign feeling in her chest, Sugar crossed her arms and leaned back into the couch.

Jackson crossed his own arms across his chest and leaned back too, their shoulders touching. "I guess you've heard some things people have been saying since Thanksgiving too," he said.

Sugar snorted as she saw one of the kittens had left Violet to scope out the new tree in the corner.

"That would be putting it mildly," she said. "It seems everyone in this town is worried about my well-being, or at least wanted to see the look on my face when they told me I shouldn't get too attached to you."

"Look, Sugar, I'm not going to pretend I've been a saint," Jackson said, turning and looking at her intently.

Sugar raised her chin and leveled her gaze at him. "Neither have I," she said defiantly.

His face softened. "Would you let me finish? What they're saying is true. I didn't have any desire to settle down, get serious, which is why I didn't get involved with women who had children. I've always been up-front about it, because a child doesn't understand why someone is in their life one minute and then gone the next."

Sugar tucked her long legs underneath her and propped her elbow on the back of the couch, resting her head in her hand. "You don't owe me any explanations, and as a single mother, I appreciate that," she said. "You've been nothing but a good friend. I was the one that took it to a different level, and like I said, I'm sorry and it won't happen again."

"That's not what I'm trying to say," Jackson said, running his hands through his hair in frustration.

She stood up and offered Jackson her hand. "It's late. We're both tired and have a busy day tomorrow."

Sighing, he took her hand and didn't let go until she handed him his coat. Sugar laced her fingers together in front of her as he put his coat on, his eyes never leaving her. *Well this is awkward*, she thought. Having a conversation about this is the whole reason she'd been kicking herself since the day she kissed him.

"Thank you again for this," she said, gesturing toward the tree. "Violet will never forget today, and neither will I. You're a good friend."

"You're welcome," he said as he zipped up his coat and walked to the door, Sugar following beside him.

As they reached the door, he turned to her. "Have I ever told you that I wanted a fling or that I didn't want to get serious because of Violet?" he asked, searching her face.

"Well no," she said as her brows knitted together in puzzlement.

Before she knew it, his arms were around her and his face was inches from hers. He waited a second to see if she'd pull away, and when she didn't, he kissed her painfully slow, his mouth gently teasing her.

Sugar hungrily pushed her body into his as her arms circled his neck. He deepened the kiss, and just when Sugar was sure she would lose her mind, he broke it off.

"Listen to me, and listen good," he said, his forehead leaning on hers as he got his breathing under control. "I'm not sorry, and I plan on doing that again. Frequently."

With that he opened the door and left, leaving a dumbfounded Sugar in his wake.

Chapter 9

"AND HE LEFT HIS DAMN DOG HERE," Sugar said as she took out her frustrations on the big ball of dough in front of her. "AND I'm pretty sure he did that on purpose."

Thanking the heavens that Emery was back, Sugar described the current situation to her best friend. Jackson had returned early the next morning, apologizing for leaving Thor there, but his annoyingly sexy grin told Sugar he was not sorry, not one bit.

Violet was thrilled to see Jackson was there when she woke up, and she danced merrily around the living room as he put the tree into the tree stand. He needed to get back to the hotel, but he didn't leave without sneaking another mind-blowing kiss.

Sugar and Violet had spent all morning decorating the tree. White lights twinkled against the huge Santa Claus ornaments Violet had seen in town and instantly loved.

Emery brought a fist up to her face, but even if she was hiding her grin, her smiling eyes gave her jovial mood away. "I think it's sweet," Emery said, "even if you think it's unnecessary, someone watching your back is not a bad idea while the TV show airs, you know, just in case."

Grabbing a large stainless-steel bowl, Sugar plopped the bread dough into it, covered it, and put it in the oven to proof. Her mom and Eric were coming over to watch this week's episode, and she had volunteered to cook dinner as usual.

It was nothing that put her out, but she missed her mom. Just her mom. Becca and Eric had been attached at the hip since they found each other again, and even though she was happy her mom was happy, she missed the days when it was just them.

Sugar rolled her eyes at Emery and proceeded to dice up the potatoes. "Just tell me what I'm supposed to do about this," she said as she put down the knife and placed her hand on her hip.

Emery tapped her long red fingernails on her closed laptop, which was surrounded by crumpled up pieces of paper from their earlier phone conference with the team. "I don't know, enjoy it? Be happy? There is a nice, kind man—who happens to be gorgeous—being incredibly sweet to you. You're going to have to face the fact that you have a boyfriend."

"I do not," Sugar said making a face. "I'm going to grow into an old eccentric lady. I already have the cats." She noticed said cats were now sneaking back into the Christmas tree.

"Branch, Smidge, get down!" she yelled. They temporarily stopped their climb of the Christmas tree, looked at Sugar, and proceeded to continue doing what they were doing, knocking ornaments off as they went.

Realizing it was a lost cause, Sugar returned to dicing potatoes. "What was I thinking? Getting a big Christmas tree when we just adopted two kittens?" she asked. "I wonder if there is, like, an electric fence you can get for trees."

"Oh no you don't," Emery interjected. "You are not pulling a Sugar and changing the subject. What is wrong with starting a relationship with Jackson? That's obviously what he was trying to say to you."

"I'm not good at . . ."

"Don't. Don't even bring out that tired old excuse," Emery said, holding her hand up like a crossing guard.

"There's a lot going on right now. The bakery, sugar-jones.com, the whole new-to-me family situation. There are just too many plates spinning in the air."

So much was happening in her life right now. Having Jackson fluster her every time he came in the vicinity of her was not helping matters.

"Plate spinning is your specialty," Emery pointed out. "Look, I know you have issues with the whole relationship stuff, but do you know how lucky you are? Do you know how many people wish they could find a connection like that?"

Sugar looked up at her friend who was suddenly interested in her nails. Emery had only returned to Snow Valley that morning and spent the morning with Violet decorating the tree. Once Violet left for her Sunday afternoon swim with Becca and Eric, they had only talked business until now.

"What's up with you?" Sugar asked, raising her eyebrows.

"Nothing," she said but sounded unsure of herself. "Todd and I broke up."

"I'm sorry," Sugar said as she walked around the kitchen peninsula and hugged her friend. She saw this coming from a mile away, but she knew to Emery failure was failure, even if it was destined, and Emery couldn't stand to fail. For selfish reasons, Sugar was glad they broke up.

Todd didn't like Sugar, and Emery was always caught in the middle. It grew worse when Todd realized that if Emery needed to pick between Sugar or him, Sugar would win every single time.

Emery hugged Sugar back. "Don't be. I should have done it a long time ago. He travels for work constantly, but the minute I do, it's this big problem and his feelings should be my priority."

"Fuck that," Sugar said. She resumed her meal prep and looked at Emery thoughtfully. "At least now you can finally get it on with Alec."

Coffee almost shot out of Emery's nose as she snorted in surprise. "Alec? Are you serious? We couldn't be more different."

"Exactly," Sugar said. "Look at us. We couldn't be more different either, yet here we are. You need someone to get your nose out of that laptop, and Alec needs someone to crack the whip. You're perfect, and don't even tell me there isn't attraction there. I have eyes, you know."

Emery rolled her eyes dismissively. "He's your brother. If things went bad, it would make things way too awkward. Besides, I need to concentrate on my business right now."

Sugar smiled at her friend. "Pot, meet kettle."

"Oh, shut up," Emery said, throwing a crumpled piece of paper at her as Sugar laughed and expertly dodged it.

Between the two of them, Sugar knew Emery was the romantic. She was the one that dreamed of the fairytale wedding, the handsome prince, and the happily ever after. It was always at odds with how she thought she should be, and until the strong independent business-woman reconciled that it was okay to want to be a princess too, she was going to have troubles.

Emery was back at work on her laptop, and Sugar continued cooking, the two both working in companionable silence. It was more than once that Sugar had noticed Alec's eyes lingering a bit too long on Emery. Bringing him up was really a diversion tactic to take Emery's mind off her breakup, but now that she thought about it, those two really did fit.

Now if she could only figure out where she fit with Jackson, or why the possibilities scared the hell out of her.

℞

"Hey Poppy," Jackson greeted as he carried the last of his stuff into the big pole barn. It was time. The Snow Valley Hotel was booked solid, so taking a room for himself didn't make sense anymore. Alec moved to one of the small cabins used when distant family came to stay for an extended vacation.

As far as Jackson was concerned, he had everything he needed right here. He spent most of his downtime here anyway, working on his woodworking projects or just winding down watching a game. It was important to have a place to escape work.

He plopped the bag down on the huge bed that took up most of the space in the small bedroom. At his size, a full or queen-sized bed just wouldn't do. The walls were a plain white, which was fine with him. A warm, safe place to lay his head was all he needed.

Thor jumped on the bed and wagged his tail in approval. He got plenty of exercise running around with Jackson all day keeping everything running smoothly at the hotel, but the hotel room was too small for a big dog like him. Poppy the cat jumped up next to him and brushed her face against his, happy her friend was here.

"Are you sure you don't want one of the other cabins?" Alec asked as he brought in the box of things from the small refrigerator Jackson kept in his hotel room. Jackson watched as Alec set them on the small counter in the kitchenette, eyeing the various pictures on his new refrigerator drawn by Violet.

They were the first things he moved.

"This will work just fine," Jackson said.

"My niece is genius," Alec said with a wide smile as he pointed to them. Jackson chuckled as he quickly unloaded the contents of the box into the refrigerator and grabbed two beers, offering one to Alec.

"She is very special for sure," Jackson said as Alec took his beer and they plopped into the comfortable leather chairs.

Alec flipped up the leg rest and let out a contented groan. "I talked to Emery, by the way," he said. "She pretty much concurred with Sugar, that creepy messages come with the territory, and if there was anything alarming, their admin would let them know."

Jackson followed Sugar's wishes and didn't tell Eric, but he never said anything about Alec. The situation weighed on his mind since she first let it slip, so he shared his concerns with him.

"What do you think?" Jackson asked.

Alec slipped his beer thoughtfully. "I don't think an

extra pair of eyes on them would hurt, especially Violet going back and forth to school. Sugar's been awful careful to keep her out of the public eye, and if you take her and I pick her up, there wouldn't be a connection to Sugar if some weirdo was hanging around."

"That's what I thought too," Jackson said, relieved Alec thought the same. "How are you going to break it to her that you're picking her up every day until Christmas break?" He knew Sugar hadn't exactly agreed to him taking Violet, but he planned on just showing up. The café would be full of people and she really couldn't turn him down.

He couldn't bear it if something happened to Violet, or Sugar. They had become so important to him in such a short amount of time that it made his head spin. This wasn't how he pictured things going for him, but this is how it was.

"I'll just say, 'Sugar, I'm picking up Violet from school the next couple of weeks.' She'll say no, and I'll just tell her that I'll tell Eric about all the creeps and he'll position himself in her living room for probably years," Alec replied with a smile as he kicked back and put his arm behind his head.

Jackson shook his head and laughed.

"I grew up with Madison, so I'm good at the whole blackmail to get what you want stuff," Alec said.

Reclining in his own chair, Jackson played with the label on his beer. Even though Sugar had only been Alec's sister for a few weeks, she was still his sister. He hadn't said anything about the rumors, but Jackson knew he must have heard them by now. Lining up the driver from The Lodge to take them to get their Christmas tree was sure to confirm anyone's suspicions.

"She does like to cause some shit," Jackson said carefully. "I'm sure you heard all the crap people were talking after Thanksgiving."

"I figured that was Madison's handiwork. Just when I thought you were safe from her evil plots, you've been devirginized." Alec held his beer up to Jackson for a toast. "Welcome to the club."

Immune to her schemes in the past, this was a new experience for Jackson. Awkward moments when Madison had set her sights on him aside, Jackson counted her as part of his family, even if her brother could barely stomach her. When he first came home from Afghanistan, she was there for him, and he'd never forget it. She'd never told a single soul about any of the issues he dealt with.

He wished the two of them could get along. Jackson couldn't deny the bad things Madison did while they were growing up. Just because she was a complete nightmare during her teen years didn't make her a bad person, and Alec certainly bore the brunt of some of her ministrations back then. But for being someone who tried to be as woke as Alec, he couldn't see that Madison saw her fair share of struggles, and that she was made to feel less than by her grandfather just because she didn't take after the Larsson side of the family.

"Not so happy about that," Jackson said. "I don't understand her. Why? Why tell people that kind of gossip?"

Alec threw his arms up in frustration. "Come on, man, you know why. She's terrified you and Sugar are going to fall in love, and because she is such a heinous bitch, she assumes Sugar will be an asshole like her and use you and The Lodge to get back at her."

"That sounds exhausting."

Alec snorted. "Look, I know you two have always gotten along well, but she's really not worth the effort. I mean, she's my twin and I wish she was, but she's not. Unfortunately, I had to learn that lesson over and over the hard way."

Jackson still didn't know the complete story about Alec and Madison. When they were elementary age, the two of them were inseparable. They started fighting when they went to high school and Madison caused so much trouble, but he came home from Afghanistan to find Alec would barely speak to her.

"I really like her," Jackson said, looking pointedly at Alec.

Alec set his beer down and turned his body toward Alec. "I'll never understand why. I mean, you were gone for most of her nastiness in high school, but you have got to know what a bitch she is by now."

Jackson shook his head. "I don't mean Madison."

"I know," Alec said, flashing his infectious smile. Turning toward the big-screen TV, he picked up the remote and clicked it on. "I've known that since you first met her."

"And just how did you know?"

Alec tapped his index finger on his forehead. "Because I pay attention. This is not just a pretty face."

Picking up a small pillow from his chair, Jackson threw it at this best friend. He knew he was right. Alec seemed to float through life without a care. People loved Alec, genuinely loved him. Even the most bitter person couldn't help but smile around him. Jackson was well aware there was much more to him. Alec saw more than most because people didn't expect him to pay attention.

"Is there a problem with that?" Jackson asked slowly.

Alec stopped on a channel playing a hockey game but didn't take his eyes from the television. "Of course not. I would have beat your ass already if there were."

Jackson snorted and kicked up his feet. "Well, you would have tried."

CR

The usual suspects were gathered at Sugar's apartment, watching the another installment of *The Holiday Baking Extravaganza.* Alec and Emery laid on their stomachs on the floor with Violet sandwiched between them. Becca and Eric snuggled on the couch, while Sugar sat in her favorite chair wrapped in her favorite quilt.

After going through this a few times, Sugar was getting used to seeing herself on television. Not understanding how this couldn't be boring to other people, she could almost give a play by play on how this week's episode would go down. It had nothing to do with the fact she lived it, but with the fact that each week was the same thing. Hunter and Bob would look incredibly bad, Brittany would make an off-handed comment about Sugar's looks, and Bettie would just be over it.

She stroked ever-present Smidge as Branch peered at her from his perch in the tree, daring her to come get him. The first round of competition had gone to jackass Bob, but Sugar knew the second round was hers again.

Bob was a talented chef, but his aesthetics always came up lacking. He refused to buy into the fact we eat with our eyes first. Sugar knew taste ruled, but they needed to entice people into wanting the food in the first place.

The judges and Tyler the host looked on at the remaining contestants, with plates of beautiful petit fours laid out before them. They praised Brittany's delicate looking packages but thought they could be more flavorful.

Bob had the opposite problem. Even though they were delicious and relatively neat, his decorations were lacking and the judges declared them boring.

Sugar stood at attention looking like a Viking warrior as Bettie and Hunter tasted her desserts. Some of the colorful bites were decorated with painstakingly perfect bows, and others with ornate piping that made them look like ornaments. Bettie closed her eyes in rhapsody as she tasted the tiramisu petit four.

Hunter took a bite, his dark eyes never leaving Sugar. "Smile, Sugar, it's not that serious," he said with a sexy grin. "You are more beautiful when you smile."

Before Sugar could answer, Bettie snapped, "And if you spoke less, you wouldn't sound like such an idiot. Sugar, these are absolutely perfect. You have been listening to the critiques and getting better and better each week."

The show cut to the confessional showing a frustrated Sugar. "Smile . . . okay," she deadpanned as she used both pixelated middle fingers to raise the corners of her mouth.

"Did you see the look on Bob's face when you won the round?" Emery asked. Violet was fast asleep, and everyone had decided to stay a bit and have some hot cocoa.

"Don't even get me started on him," Sugar said.

The whole competition he zeroed in on Sugar, from the very first meet and greet. He was a jerk both on and off camera, and now that Sugar was older, she knew it was because she intimidated him. Bob the asshole couldn't bring himself to admit a woman was better than him.

"I'd like five minutes alone with him," Eric grumbled as he massaged Becca's shoulder.

The last thing Sugar needed was someone to defend her, but she appreciated the gesture. "Eh, I've dealt with worse. People like him just can't help it. The more you feed into it, the more they get off on it."

Emery turned her cell phone to the group. "Hunter's really taking a beating on social media. I can't believe the show is making him look this bad. Usually with editing they try to make their own stars look good."

Getting up to pick up the wayward Santa Claus ornaments, Sugar thought about this. Hunter really wasn't bad. Off camera, he was focused and aloof, but she wouldn't count him in the Neanderthal category. Both of his restaurants had female head chefs. Men stuck in the fifties didn't put women in charge of big operations like that.

"One thing is for sure," Becca said as she came back into the room from the kitchen, carrying a plate of Sugar's cookies. "Bettie isn't having it."

Snapping up one of the cookies, Eric chuckled. "She reminds me of Mrs. McNamby."

Sugar, Alec, and Emery looked questioningly at Eric. "Mrs. McNamby was our home ec teacher," Becca explained.

"Home ec?" Alec asked.

Eric chuckled. "We are officially old, Becks." Making his voice sound gravely, he hunched over. "You see, children, back in the day, part of our education was cooking and sewing and all things home. Mrs. McNamby was a no-nonsense lady who didn't take crap from anyone and didn't appreciate it when she caught you making out in the pantry."

Becca laughed and slapped at Eric's arm as it went

around her. A big smile sprouted on Sugar's face. "So my mother got caught making out at school?"

Eric wiggled his eyebrows. "Constantly."

It was so strange for Sugar to think of her mom having a life before her. She guessed it was probably like that for everyone, but considering how secretive her mom was about her early life, Sugar never pictured part of it might be happy. All she ever knew was she never wanted to go back home, and even if it was a little gross thinking about her mom and Eric making out, it made her glad to know there were in fact happy moments.

Becca cuddled into Eric more and slapped his arm again. "Enough with the confessions," she said. "Don't forget we are going dress shopping Wednesday, you two," she said to Sugar and Emery.

The wedding was going to be small and private. Becca and Eric had opted for a simple wedding on Christmas Day with their families. Eric already did the big, formal wedding with Allison, and Becca simply wasn't a big wedding type person.

Sugar groaned as Emery clasped her hands together. "I simply cannot wait!" Emery exclaimed.

A root canal sounded more fun to Sugar, but she placed a fake smile on her face. "How could I forget?" she asked and zoned out as Becca and Emery began discussing colors and fabrics.

Madison was going too. It was not lost on Sugar that Madison hadn't been around. Becca had insisted she invite Madison to watch the show each week, and each week Madison politely declined because she was busy. This didn't hurt Sugar's feelings at all; quite the opposite, in fact. The less time she spent with her sister the better.

Even though they reached a tentative peace, Sugar was still hesitant to get closer to her sister. Girls like her made her life a living hell when she was growing up, and while most girls grow out of that mean girl phase, Madison obviously hadn't.

It didn't matter how she felt about Madison. She was part of the package with Eric, and now that he was a part of her life and marrying her mom, Sugar had no choice but to deal with it.

Chapter 10

"**WATCH THIS, JACKSON!**" Violet squealed as she raced to the top of the hill, pulling her sled behind her.

The trio of Sugar, Violet, and Jackson was at a sledding hill behind The Lodge. True to his word, he diligently showed up every morning to take Violet to school, and when she asked Sugar to take her sledding the next day, he informed them both he knew the perfect place, so here they were.

Even though she loved the café with all her heart, it was good to be outside and active. She knew it was just the time of year that made everything so busy and chaotic, but Sugar knew she needed to work on the work/life balance thing. Every day seemed to bring a new first for Violet, and she didn't want to miss a minute of it by working all her waking hours. She was lucky to be in a position where she didn't need to work round the clock anymore.

Breathing in the fresh air, she couldn't help but admit this was the perfect sledding hill. It was a short walk from the main hotel and was big enough to be thrilling, but not so big that she worried about how fast Violet would go. With the smell of pine and fresh air filling her senses and the breathtaking view of the mountains, Sugar felt peaceful and invigorated at the same time. She didn't even mind the cold for once.

With a mischievous smile on her lips, she scooped up a ball of snow and gauged her target, hitting Jackson squarely in the back.

He spun around quickly, aqua blue eyes dancing. "Don't make out a check your ass can't cash," he warned.

Sugar chuckled while squatting down and gathering more snow. "Don't make out a check your ass can't cash," she mimicked with a fake deep tone. "What are you, fifty?"

"Here I go, Mommy!" Violet shrieked as she boarded her shiny red sled Eric bought for her. Sugar smiled and shielded her eyes, always happy when Violet forgot to call her Mom instead of Mommy.

A temporary truce to their snowball war didn't need to be said as they watched Violet sled down the hill, laughing and hollering the whole way. Once she reached the bottom, Violet turned to watch the other kids come down the hill, having made fast friends with the children staying at the hotel.

Smack. Sugar landed a solid hit to Jackson's left shoulder, the broken pieces of the snowball hitting him in the face.

Shit, Sugar thought as he turned with a devious look on his face, a slow, sexy smile crossing his lips. His long legs started to close the distance between them, but Sugar had long legs too. She sprinted in the other direction toward the hill, but it was in vain. Jackson caught up easily, his arms encircling her waist, lifting her from the ground like she was a small child.

"I'm coming, Mommy!" Violet called as she scooped up her own snowball, hitting Sugar square in the stomach.

"You best just have bad aim, child," Sugar laughed as Jackson unceremoniously dumped her into a snowbank.

"Get her!" Jackson exclaimed as Violet jumped on her mother and they both started pounding her with snow.

"I was in labor with you for seven hours, you ingrate," Sugar screeched as she put her hands up to protect her face from the onslaught.

"Come on, Violet, let's go again!" a little girl called. Violet jumped up to run to her new friends as Sugar swatted at her little butt. She laughed merrily as she grabbed her sled and ran to the hill.

Sugar made a small snowball and half-heartedly threw it at Jackson's leg. "You turned my own child against me," she pouted.

"I did warn you," he pointed out.

Never in a million years would Sugar think sitting in a snowbank on a cold December day would be the perfect place to be. It always warmed her heart to see her little girl making friends so readily, and Jackson being here wasn't half bad either.

"She's fearless," he said with a big smile on his face and clapping as Violet went down the hill backward on her sled.

"That she is," Sugar sighed as she plopped back down on the snowbank, looking up at the perfect blue sky. Big, puffy clouds floated by as her mind began to decipher them into shapes, still keeping an eye on Violet who was racing up the hill again. She would be out like a light once she got in the car.

Jackson sat back on his elbows, looking up at the sky

with Sugar. "That one looks like an elephant," she said, pointing to a rather rotund cloud.

"Or an ornament," Jackson said. "It is Christmas time, you know."

Sugar smiled a big smile as Violet held hands with a little girl and a little boy as they tried a joint sled down the hill. "It's so easy for her."

Turning his body slightly toward Sugar, he raised an eyebrow. "What is?"

Propping herself up on her own elbows, Sugar nodded. "Making friends. You fear a lot of things, well everything, when you have a kid, but her not getting along with other kids was in the top five."

Jackson took Sugar's gloved hand in his. "Didn't you have a lot of friends growing up?" he asked gently.

"Not when I was her age," Sugar said with a sad smile. "Until I met Emery, I never had any friends. The other kids hated me. I was obnoxious, couldn't wait my turn, talked over people. It wasn't until they found out I had ADHD and got help that I was tolerable to anyone but my mom."

"Sounds lonely," Jackson said as he squeezed her hand. She looked up into his compassionate eyes and felt a warmth spread over her. He understood and wasn't pretending or saying what he thought she wanted to hear because he wanted something from her. Jackson truly cared for her.

"It was," Sugar said. Still surprised by her realization, she suddenly felt terrified. Terrified and claustrophobic.

Mashing her emotions deep down, she let go of Jackson's hand and fiddled with the scarf, loosening it around her neck. "How about you? Were you like captain of the football team?"

Jackson rested his arms on his bent knees, squinting as he looked in the distance. "No, nothing like that. I've always kept a small circle. Quality over quantity when it comes to friends. When I was really little, I always had Alec and Madison—didn't need much more than that. As we got older, you realize people want to become your friend more because of what you have than what you are. We all learned that lesson."

"I bet. There were a lot more haves than have nots where I went to school," Sugar said. "It seems a bit more disproportioned here."

"It gets more balanced when they go to high school," Jackson told her. "Several towns around here go to the same school, so there's a bigger pond, bigger fish."

Sugar nodded and shivered a little. Sitting here in the snow for so long was starting to get to her, even with her powder blue ski suit. She didn't want to admit the reason why she didn't wear the black Michelin Man coat, even though deep down she knew it was to look good for Jackson.

Standing up, Jackson took her hand again, pulling her to her feet. "What do you say we show these kids how it's done?" he asked with a wink.

Sugar smiled a slow smile, and letting go of his hand, she took off running toward the hill.

CR

Mother and daughter walked arm and arm through the big town square, heading to the local dress shop to look at dresses for the upcoming wedding. Becca knew she needed some alone time with her daughter to see how everything was going. So much had changed since she returned to her small hometown just a little over a month ago.

The wedding wasn't going to be anything fussy. There would be a small ceremony before Christmas dinner. Most of the Larsson clan would be in for the holiday, and Becca had some friends coming into town. The ceremony would be short and sweet, as it was a formality. Becca and Eric belonged to each other their whole lives, even when apart.

All this change in just over a month would make a normal person's head spin, but Becca's daughter was not normal. She always thrived on change and trying new things, but this was so much. Meeting her father, being on television, taking over the bakery, moving and dealing with new family members—it had put so much on Sugar.

Becca saw the disappointed look on her daughter's face whenever she stopped by and Eric was with her. She needed some mother-daughter time, but keeping Eric away wasn't the easiest thing in the world. After missing out on so much of her life, he was determined to not miss another minute, and Becca didn't have the heart to tell him his daughter needed time with just her.

Things would get easier with time, once Eric felt more secure in his position of father. From what she could see with his other two children, he was a fantastic father, something Becca never doubted. Dress shopping wasn't something he would share, so she took advantage of the situation and tore Sugar away from the bakery a little early to walk around town before Violet got out of school and they met Emery and Madison.

Madison was another fly in the ointment. Things did

not get off to a great start with that one. Becca had spent time with her since that first disastrous meeting between the new sisters, and she found her to be a bright, ambitious girl. Some of her personality traits made Becca uneasy, but since she was Eric's daughter, she needed to put in the effort to get to know her.

Dealing with problem after problem with girls after Sugar entered puberty, those personality traits made Sugar more than uneasy. She outright avoided her new sister, as Madison outright avoided her. Sugar and Alec took to each other like they were raised together. Alienating Madison would not help the situation and was cruel.

Walking past a colorful shop with different types of candy in the window, Becca smiled. "My father and I used to sneak over here and buy candy. Mother didn't want candy in her home, so we'd buy a couple of candy bars and go watch the skaters in the square."

"I wish I could have known him," Sugar said, peering in the window.

Becca sighed, squeezing her daughter's arm. "Me too, more than you know. What do you say we get ourselves some candy and go watch the skaters?"

"YOU? Eat candy?" Sugar said. "I'm in, and I'll mark it on the calendar."

Becca was a very health conscious person. Yoga, strength training, and clean eating had been her mantra for decades. Since she never thought it would be possible for Sugar to know her dad, she felt a deep responsibility to stay healthy for her daughter as she was her only family. A little splurge now and then wouldn't hurt, and she finally felt she could relax a bit now that her daughter was grown.

"Business is right on track," Sugar said as they sat down on the little bench on the side of the skating rink with their treats. "I just love it, really love it."

Becca smiled and watched the few skaters that were out on the rink during a weekday. The air smelled of freshly roasted chestnuts, mixed with rich hot chocolate from the stand next to it. Everywhere you looked you saw Christmas. From the candy cane striped light poles to the charming vendor stands decorated in boughs of evergreen and Christmas lights, no other place on Earth captured the magic of the season like Snow Valley in Becca's eyes. Snow was gently falling around the pair and people bustled about the small shops built around the square. No matter how hard she tried, she never could recreate this feeling in San Diego.

"That's wonderful, Sug," Becca said as she popped a soft peppermint in her mouth, closing her eyes in delight. "What about all of this?" she said as she gestured to the square in general. "Can you imagine yourself staying in this crazy little town?"

"I think I can," Sugar said as she smirked at a guy who took a tumble after trying to show off on the ice. "Violet loves it here. She's taken to the snow like a little polar bear."

Becca couldn't argue with that. Her little granddaughter positively thrived here. Sledding, ice skating, and skiing, Violet loved all the winter sports living in this small mountain town afforded. She'd already made many friends at school and welcomed her newfound family with open arms and heart.

"She sure has," Becca said. "She even has her own bodyguards it seems." She was dying to bring up the subject of Jackson. Becca wasn't blind and saw the way he looked at her daughter. When the rumor mill started talking about Jackson taking Violet to school every day, and less so about Alec picking her up, Becca knew something was up.

"Oh, they're just helping me out because we're so busy," Sugar said slowly, dismissing the bodyguard comment with a wave.

Becca patted her daughter's arm. "Tell that story to someone who doesn't know better," she said as she squinted her eyes at her stubborn daughter.

Sugar sighed and leaned forward, resting her arms on her knees, suddenly interested in the skaters. "Fine, but you can't tell Eric."

"I'm about to marry your dad, Sugar, and we don't keep secrets," Becca admonished.

Sitting back up, Sugar looked into her mother's eyes. "Alright, then just refrain from telling him?"

Becca shook her head. "I make no such promise."

Standing up, Sugar took her mother's hand to pull her up. "We better get going. Don't want to be late for dress shopping!" she said with mock excitement.

Becca took her daughter's hand and pulled her back down on the bench with a yank. "Nope."

Sugar groaned and pulled her hand from her mom's. "Alright, alright. I stupidly said something about the creepy messages I sometimes get when explaining why I won't let Violet's picture be online, and those two suddenly think I need bodyguards. They've settled for taking Violet back and forth to school."

Becca twisted so she could look at her daughter head on. "Is there anything to worry about?"

Rolling her big blue eyes, Sugar shook her head. "Nothing that doesn't come with the territory. Vanessa is vetting everything and would let me know if there's anything troubling. Well, more troubling than normal."

Vanessa was Sugar's admin at sugarjones.com, and Becca knew the woman was very good at her job. She was the iron fortress behind the company, and probably just as protective as Becca was of Sugar. A foster child who had been turned out on the streets at eighteen, she was eternally grateful to Sugar and Emery for giving her a chance all those years ago and would do anything in the world for them.

"If you say there's nothing to worry about, then I believe you," Becca said. "I'm sure your brother and Jackson's hearts are in the right place."

This time Becca stood and pulled her daughter up, smiling at her daughter's groan. Shopping wasn't at the top of Sugar's favorite activities. If Becca had to guess, it was right above going to the dentist. She heard her daughter's cell phone alarm go off.

Sugar took out her cell phone and Becca watched her swipe the "Pick up Violet from school" alarm and sighed. She wished her daughter had more confidence in herself and didn't set all the silly little alarms, but if it gave her peace of mind, who was she to say anything?

"Jackson and Alec could never understand," Sugar said as they walked arm and arm across the square, smiling and nodding at people they knew. "For one, they grew up here. Secondly, they have penises. Alec threatened to tell Eric about it all, that's why I'm allowing it. Jerk."

Becca laughed. "Oh my, what a horrible brother, looking out for his baby sister and niece."

They were nearing the school, so she broke out the big guns. "So, Jackson and you seem to be getting along really well," she said.

"Mom. Stop," Sugar said. Becca knew it wasn't her imagination when Sugar picked up their leisurely pace, and Becca purposefully slowed them down.

"Stop what?" she said innocently. "Your dad says Jackson is a really good man."

When Sugar just shook her head, Becca squeezed her arm. "I'm your mother. I don't care how old you get or how many children you have, it is my job to ask about these things."

"Ugh, alright, alright," Sugar said, holding her hands up in surrender. "He is a good man, and he's really good to Violet. She loves him. There are a lot of factors at play right now, and I'm just trying to get through one change at a time."

Putting her arm around her daughter's shoulder, she gave her a good squeeze. "I know you've been through a lot. Just keep an open mind. I want my daughter to be happy."

They reached the outside of the preschool, with the same shiny gray stone as the rest of the buildings on the square. Kids were lining up, dressed in their winter gear waiting to be picked up. A long line of vehicles stretched the length of the road, but Becca and Sugar sidestepped all that to go and pick up Violet since they were walking.

She was standing in line animatedly gesturing while relaying some story to a few friends who were giggling behind their colorful mittens. A wide, dazzling smile erupted on Sugar's face. "That," she said pointing at Violet, "is what makes me happy."

"Me too," said Becca as she waved at her granddaughter, "but other things can make you happy as well."

"Noted," said Sugar as she bent down on one knee to hug her daughter as she came running to greet them.

Becca knew that would have to be enough for now, and she wouldn't push it. Pushing Sugar never did any bit of good, and she needed to realize things in her own time. She just hoped she would.

℘

Madison followed Sugar up the stairs to her little apartment above the bakery. She wanted to kill her father for this. One of their biggest clients, a pop star who liked getting out of the limelight with her family many times a year, was also a huge fan of *The Holiday Baking Extravaganza*.

As far as exclusive guests, she was one of the better ones. Like most who rented the luxury cabins on the back lots of their property, she rolled in with her own entourage, not wanting to take a chance that a strange cook or maid might spy on her. Madison never met the woman and wouldn't even know who she was, except she spotted her one time in the summer. She dealt with her PA, which was fine with her.

Sometimes they would get requests from these guests, or a random complaint. For the most part, these were the easiest clients, because making sure the 4,000 square foot cabins were perfect and clean when they arrived was the only task needed done by The Lodge.

The PA hunted Madison down the minute they arrived and let her know her boss was a huge fan of the show and of Sugar. The star wanted to try some of the items Sugar made on the show, but of course didn't want to go into town.

Emery had used the Sugar Jones brand to get visibility for not only the small offshoot her idiot brother started but also The Lodge. Even though she never said it out loud, Madison knew it helped both ventures. The Lodge was a luxury resort, but it did have rooms in the price range attainable for upper middle-class people. Many who didn't know about it were booking now.

It was only natural to task Eric to get the baked goods for their prized client, and he promptly told her to get them herself. Aware of the reason why, Madison didn't have a choice but to ask.

While Becca tried on wedding gowns, Madison bit the bullet and inquired about it. To her surprise, Sugar said she could give her the desserts made last week, along with the ones from the show that wouldn't be aired until tomorrow next week.

Madison expected her half-sister to make her grovel, especially after how they first met. She didn't go to the family dinner to introduce Sugar to the family, so when she ran into her at The Lodge after Sugar was leaving a spa treatment, she assumed the worst—that Sugar and her mother were after the Larsson money.

Any other time the rumor mill in town could be counted on to give the juicy facts, but this time it let her down. Madison didn't know about Becca's success as a writer or Sugar's own juggernaut of a company.

She so much as accused Sugar of going after her father's money, which made both Sugar and her friend Emery upset. Madison looked like a damn fool, and there was nothing worse in her mind. The thought of it still brought heat to Madison's cheeks.

"Aunt Madison, I can't wait to show you my crowns," little Violet said as Sugar struggled with the deadbolt on the door.

"Let her get inside first, monkey," Sugar said as she finally jiggled the door open and typed in her security code on the keypad.

Madison didn't have much interaction with her new-found sister, but she spent a bit of time with her little niece when she visited Eric or Becca at The Lodge. A bright little girl with a sweet disposition, she won Madison's heart from the start.

The apartment was incredibly small but nicely furnished in a tasteful French country style. Madison's bedroom at The Lodge was probably bigger than the main living area and kitchen combined. Surely Eric had offered up one of the smaller guest cabins they kept in the area reserved just for family. Perhaps she just stayed here because it was easier with Violet.

"Be right back!" Violet shouted as she ran to what Madison assumed was her bedroom, leaving Madison and Sugar alone.

"I think I have some of last week's up here, but I'll have to go downstairs to the bakery to get this Sunday's items," Sugar said as she hung up her coat. She went into the kitchen and Madison dutifully followed.

After an awkward silence, Madison noticed cooking utensils lined up on the island separating the kitchen from the living area. They were all embossed with the Sugar Jones LLC logo. She walked over and picked up a metal measuring cup.

"That's all Emery," Sugar sighed as she opened a container. "She's working on a deal to partner with some company to produce a line for Sugar Jones."

Madison may have nothing in common with Sugar and not know what to say, but business—business she could talk.

"Emery certainly is good at what she does," Madison said, admiring the craftmanship of the utensils. These were not cheap, plastic measuring spoons, cups, and spatulas. These were a rose gold metal and the design was gorgeous, making them more a work of art than a kitchen utensil. "How did you start your business?" she asked as she took a seat on one of the stools in front of the island.

Sugar searched through one of her cabinets and brought down three more containers containing treats. She opened a box emblazoned with the Sugar Jones logo and started filling it up.

"Do you want anything to drink?" Sugar asked and Madison shook her head no. "Well, we were fifteen and YouTube and Facebook were just starting to blow up. Emery and I set up a little cupcake stand at the local farmer's market when we were like twelve, and by the time I was fifteen, I was pretty freaking good at decorating cupcakes."

Madison took her coat off and hung it on the stool next to her, impressed they were so ambitious at such a young age.

"Josh, Emery, and I had been friends forever, and we decided we were going to be these big YouTube people. My mom wasn't having it, and only agreed when we said we would just show my hands. Since we couldn't do a cooking show type deal, Josh decided to fast forward it, and boom, it went crazy almost as soon as we posted the first video." Sugar smiled. "Emery had the marketing ability, Josh had the computer skills, and I knew my way around an oven. We were prepared, and we kept leveling up."

Madison smiled. "And here you are, with measuring cups stamped with your name."

Sugar laughed. "Not my idea, I assure you. We have to get it while we can. You never know when public opinion will change, or something new comes along."

"Aunt Madison, come see my crowns!" Violet said as she lugged a big wooden box out of her room.

"Do you mind staying up here with her while I run down and get the desserts from next week's show?" Sugar asked as she set the other desserts on the counter.

Madison nodded in the affirmative and smiled at her excited niece, who was now pulling crowns out of the big wooden box and gently setting them on the coffee table in the living room.

"This one is my favorite," Violet said, placing the crown atop her curly blonde head. It was shiny silver with violet shaped rhinestones at each peak.

Sugar had brought the desserts for next week's show upstairs, but they were having a problem in the bakery. Madison was having such a good time with her niece that she told Sugar to go take care of it. Staying with Violet was the least she could do since Sugar's collection of desserts would undoubtedly make The Lodge's popstar client happy.

She sat there now with her own ruby red and gold crown and red feathered boa. "I have clip-on earrings that match. Be right back!" Violet exclaimed as she raced back into her room.

As Violet left, Madison's phone sprang to life, and she sighed as soon as the name glared across the screen.

Carrie.

Almost everyone Madison knew communicated simple things with text, but not Carrie. She almost exclusively called because she didn't want a written record of anything she said, or at least that's how Madison saw it.

The girl could be useful when Madison wanted to spread information, but for the most part, she didn't like her. They'd known each other since high school, and since Carrie came from an affluent family a few towns away, they ran in the same circles.

Carrie's family owned a construction and design firm. She couldn't ignore her call because they were planning their big annual Christmas party at The Lodge that year. It was a huge score for The Lodge, and like it or not, she needed to keep her happy. Taking a deep breath and squaring her shoulders, she answered the call.

After listening to her drone on and on about how their party needed to be the party of the year, Madison finally found a moment to break into the conversation. "I'm sure we'll do everything possible to make this the best holiday party ever, but I really need to go. I'm watching my niece and she needs me," she lied as Violet had once again raced to her room to find another one of her treasures to show Madison.

"Really . . ." Carrie said as Madison internally kicked herself. She had just given her an opening to gossip about Sugar and Jackson. Deep down Madison knew she had no one to blame but herself for starting the whole Sugar and Jackson business in the first place.

"From what I've heard, Jackson seems to be changing his stripes," Carrie cooed into the phone. "He's even taking the little girl to school every day."

Madison overheard a conversation between Jackson and Alec about Sugar having some creepy fans, so she knew that was probably why. No one ever brought up the fact that Alec picked her up. She wanted to tell her as much but kept her mouth shut. Madison wasn't stupid and she knew Becca and Sugar were not going to stand for her games.

The living room now looked like every little girl's fantasy as Violet came out of her room in a light pink princess dress and little heels. Madison smiled at her and gave her a thumbs-up.

"You know Jackson, he's a nice guy that helps everyone," Madison said.

"That's more than being nice," Carrie said as Madison pictured her rolling her eyes. "I wouldn't be surprised if your family had a second wedding to plan this year."

It shouldn't have bothered her as much as it did, but the thought of Jackson and Sugar marrying stung. As far as Madison could tell, Sugar did nothing to try and get his attention, and Madison had done everything in her power to get his attention back in the day. It just hit that spot of insecurity that always resonated with her about not being the perfect blonde, tall daughter.

Conscious of the fact that Violet was in the room, she minded her words. "Jackson would never marry S-U-G-A-R. He doesn't like K-I-D-S."

Sugar re-entered the apartment at that moment and

Madison hastily said her goodbyes to get Carrie off the phone.

"It's almost time for dinner, Violet," Sugar announced as she walked into the living room. "Get this all picked up, okay?"

"Okay," Violet said in a small voice as she looked at the ground.

Madison felt her stomach drop as Sugar looked questioningly at her. What if the little girl could spell? She shrugged her shoulders but couldn't help but feel the panic rise. Besides the fact that she wouldn't want to hurt the little girl, there would be ramifications in her family.

"What's wrong, Violet?" she asked as Violet shook her head and started packing up the various dress-up accessories.

"Nothing," Violet said as she kept working.

"I'm sorry to grab and run, but I need to get back to work," Madison said as she put her coat on and gathered up the boxes Sugar had stacked on the kitchen island. "I really do appreciate this," she said sincerely.

"Anytime," Sugar said as she walked Madison to the door.

She stood outside on the small landing, looking down the stairs leading to the alley behind the bakery. Maybe she should go back in and say something. Kids have short attention spans, right? Violet would probably be on to the next thing before Madison could get down the stairs.

With a pit in her stomach, she walked down the stairs, hoping she hadn't made a really big mistake.

Chapter 11

VIOLET KEPT QUIET about what she heard Madison say until bedtime. Sugar knew she would get around to telling her, and it took all her strength not to hop in the car and wring Madison's tiny neck. Mostly she felt like a damn fool for trusting her in the first place.

Instead of reacting, she took a deep breath and assessed the situation. This could go bad, really bad. Sugar was a mother bear to her very core, but she was nothing compared to Becca. She saw that firsthand her freshman year of high school. Back then, Becca went for blood and didn't stop until she got it. Super nice people are the most dangerous when enraged.

With no other option, she decided to tell Jackson. Little Violet's lip quivered when she said Jackson didn't like her and didn't like her mom because of her. Through big fat tears, Sugar learned what happened, or at least how a four-year-old perceived it. Sugar wanted no doubt to remain in her little girl's head about Jackson.

Even with thinking the situation through, she forgot one little detail: Jackson was one of those super nice people, and Jackson was now super enraged.

Sugar simply texted him that night, asking if he wanted to do breakfast the next day. Without hesitation, he texted back, and as Violet dressed the next morning, she explained what happened the night before.

Pure anger flashed out of his aqua blue eyes and dissipated as soon as Violet came into the room. He sat her down and explained how she was one of his favorite people, and how if he could pick any child in the world to be his, it would be her.

Tears still threatened to erupt from her eyes when she thought about it. He didn't say it to appease Violet; he meant it.

The town's children were building Swedish snow lanterns in the square, and he tagged along. Patiently he helped Violet make all her snowballs the same size and place them in a ring, building a smaller ring on top of each until it formed a snowball pyramid. That night tealights would be put in, lighting up the town square.

Jackson invited the two of them to snowshoe one of the trails at The Lodge, and after being around so many people, Sugar was excited about peace and quiet. What started out as a simple breakfast turned into an all-day affair.

It didn't take long for both Sugar and Violet to catch on to the new sport. Jackson told her if you could walk, you could snowshoe, and he was right. The fresh air was invigorating, and the scenery breathtaking. With pine trees tipped with fresh fallen snow and a temperature hovering just under freezing, it was the perfect day.

Jackson was patient as they went along the trail, slowly moving so Violet's little legs could keep up. For the millionth time, Sugar wondered about the source of his never-ending patience. He chose a trail that was already packed and relatively flat for their maiden voyage.

The roar of a snowmobile in the distance broke through the peaceful quiet. Sugar turned her head to see one of The Lodge's sleds heading straight toward them. Slowing down as it neared them, the driver removed his helmet to reveal a smiling Alec.

The trio scooted over to the sled as Alec shut off the engine and produced a small helmet covered in violets. Sugar shook her head. Thinking they'd use the rental equipment when they arrived at the trails, she was surprised to find Eric had already purchased outdoor gear for both herself and Violet. She shouldn't have been surprised he had a helmet ready for Violet, and she knew there was probably one for her back at The Lodge.

"Hey squirt," Alec said, lifting Violet off the ground. He gave her a big bear hug and gnawed on her shoulder, causing her to giggle. "What do you say we ditch these two and go for a little ride?"

Violet's little mouth made an "O" as she whipped her head to her mother. Alec copied her face, and Sugar couldn't help but laugh.

"Oh, please, Mommy, please, pleeeease can I go for a ride?"

"I don't know," Sugar said doubtfully. She couldn't help but feel Alec showed up just to give her some alone time with Jackson.

"It's perfectly safe," Alec said as he put Violet back on the ground, handing her the helmet. Violet eagerly put it on, slamming down the face shield. "I promise I'll go slow. Pleeeease?"

Sugar relented and waved as she watched the two of

them slowly whoosh away on the open trail. After a few minutes, the peaceful quiet returned, and the couple resumed their snow filled hike at a much faster pace. The fresh air and strenuous activity invigorated Sugar, and the beautiful setting calmed her ever racing mind.

Being alone with Jackson awoke the butterflies in her stomach. Sugar could get used to days like this, and as much as she hated to admit it, she liked just being there with him. He had this smell—like the fresh outdoors and pine and spice, and he was just such a man. She knew in today's day and age she wasn't supposed to say she needed one, but she sure wanted one right now.

"I can't believe she'd say something like that in front of her," Jackson said, his voice starting to boil again.

"I doubt she knew a four-year-old could spell," Sugar pointed out, "and most kids wouldn't have got the *kid* word. Her dad was smart like that." Violet was a bright little girl, and she knew Sugar's name. She already knew many sight words before school, and since starting preschool, she absorbed information like a sponge.

Jackson pushed off with one of his poles in frustration. "That's no excuse. She shouldn't have been talking about that in the first place. The only other person who'd surprise me more by sticking up for her would be Alec."

Sugar reached over and gave his shoulder a little push. "I'm not making excuses or sticking up for her. It's just the truth. Trust me, if I thought it was malicious, this would have ended with me in prison. Normally I am all about ripping the Band-Aid off and calling people out, but now is not the time. I don't want anything to mess up the wedding and trust me when I say you don't want to see Becca Jones pissed."

A low rumble of a laugh escaped from Jackson. "You keep saying that, but I can't imagine your mother hurting a fly. She might be the nicest person I've ever met in my life."

The tone of his laughter had her butterflies turning into bats, but Sugar knew he was right. Becca was genuinely nice and didn't have a mean bone in her body. Unusually compassionate, people sought Becca out for advice or when they needed someone to listen. Patient and kind, people gravitated to her.

Stabbing her poles into the snow, she stopped and placed her hands on her hips. "What if I told you she went after a fifteen-year-old girl with the fury of a thousand burning suns?"

Jackson stopped and turned Sugar's direction. "I can't imagine that happening."

Sugar pushed off hard, picking up the pace in her stride. "Well, it happened. This bitch I went to school with, Amanda Miller, had this hatred for me. Intense hatred. I never did anything to her and avoided anything that had to do with her at all costs."

The trail suddenly felt claustrophobic, and Sugar pushed herself harder as she continued her story. "My mom tried talking to her parents, but they were just as awful. They believed kids will be kids and I should learn how to defend myself. It wasn't ever going to change."

Jackson kept pace with Sugar, listening to her every word. He didn't interject anything, seemingly knowing she needed to get this all out in one fell swoop.

"So one day at school, the police locked us down. Everyone was terrified an active shooter or something was on the loose. It turns out there was child pornography being spread by students, and as I would find out later, I was the star."

"Jesus, Sug," Jackson said as he let out a slow breath.

Slowing her pace, Sugar came to a stop. "It was a locker room pic. It was a side shot and I was holding a towel, thank God, but it had side boob and the curve of my ass. A concerned classmate told Emery, who called her dad, Avery, who's a lawyer, who called some judge friends and my mom. The cops were involved, and everything was locked down."

Jackson went to Sugar and gently took her into his arms, his cheek resting on the top of her head as she leaned into him, that scent giving her the confidence to continue.

Sugar pulled back but stayed in the safety of his arms. She looked up into his compassionate blue eyes and continued. "They called the kids with the picture in, one by one, and with the threat of being a labeled sex offender for the rest of their lives, they promptly told on the person who sent it to them until they got to ground zero, Amanda Miller. She was responsible for taking the picture and spreading it around."

Kissing the top of her head, Jackson pulled her in for another hug. "That had to be terrible."

"It was," she said as she pulled free from his grasp. "Becca didn't let up until Amanda was in juvie. I mean, she went for that girl's blood even with people telling her she was just a kid that made a mistake. Becca wasn't having it. I never set foot in that school again. She let me homeschool, and I finished high school before I turned sixteen."

It counted as one of the most devastating and

embarrassing moments of Sugar's young life. The thought of half the school seeing her semi-naked was humiliating. Sometimes Sugar wished she'd returned to school, wished they didn't break her.

Despite Amanda being in juvie, Sugar knew the boys at school would just use the picture as another reason to grab at her, even if it was taken without her knowledge. Sugar silently thanked the heavens for Emery for the millionth time. She always knew how to handle situations.

Not able to remember the last time she spoke of this, Sugar was surprised she spilled the whole thing to Jackson. He was a good listener and Sugar knew he had his own demons as well. She hoped someday he felt comfortable enough to share them with her.

They picked up the pace and came to the end of the trail that opened into a clearing set up for a picnic area for the warmer months. Alec and Violet were there, currently making snow angels. Sugar took a deep breath, filling her lungs with the fresh, clean mountain air.

"I usually don't tell people about that," Sugar said as she watched her daughter playing with her uncle. She didn't know why, but telling Jackson the story lifted a burden off her shoulders.

"I'm glad you told me," Jackson said sincerely.

Sugar smiled. "Me too."

With a weight off her shoulders, she took in the beauty around her. The understanding, honest man beside her, little Violet and Alec laughing as they made snow angels, the breathtaking mountain view, and the seemingly endless snowflakes falling all around them. For the first time since moving here, she thought maybe, just maybe, this might be home.

CR

"I don't like this," Sugar said as she smoothed down her close-fitting red wool cable-knit sweater. Ever relentless, Emery planned a finale party at the Snow Valley Hotel. Although she was glad to help Jackson and Alec, watching herself on television was hard enough, much less in a room full of people.

"I know," Emery said as she fixed her eyeliner in the mirror. "It's not just about business, Sug. Everyone wants to celebrate with you. There are a lot of people who care about you around here, you know."

Sugar fluffed her long hair, which was loose with beachy waves. The two friends were in the small bathroom in the lobby of the Snow Valley Hotel. Violet already made a beeline to her grandma and grandpa, and the two friends were doing a last-minute check before they joined the guests in the big rec room.

Emery looked downright festive in a pair of red skinny jeans and a loose fitting red and green striped silk button down shirt. The rips in Sugar's skinny jeans showed off red and white striped leggings, and she looked just as festive, if not in a more casual way.

As they walked into the lobby, Emery took out her phone, holding it up in the air for a selfie. The two friends both made funny faces, and she snapped the photo. "Now smile," Emery commanded, and Sugar obeyed, knowing she'd be there forever and a day until Emery got one she liked for the Sugar Jones social media accounts.

"When are your parents getting in?" Sugar asked. Emery's parents were very different than Becca, but

Sugar loved them just the same. They were coming in for Becca and Eric's wedding and were staying for Christmas. Sugar's parents were putting them up in one of the executive suites at The Lodge, and Emery decided to stay with them over the holiday.

"The twenty-third," Emery said as they walked down the hallway leading to the rec room. "They're excited about having snow for Christmas. Speaking of which, are you all set in that department?"

Sugar rolled her ice blue eyes. "Yes, Mother. In fact, you'll be proud to know everything has been delivered and wrapped."

Emery stopped short. "It's the end of days, isn't it?" she said seriously.

Sugar laughed and linked arms with Emery. "Miracles happen, Em, every day. I'm just waiting on Violet's *Trolls* Lego set. Of course, the one thing she wants more than anything is a discontinued toy. Vanessa found one on eBay."

"We need to give that girl a raise," Emery said as she stopped in front of the doors to the rec room. "You ready for this?"

Sugar nodded and they walked through the doors as applause filled the air. The large stone fireplace roared with red and orange flames as people came up to congratulate Sugar on her progress so far in the competition. Everyone was there. Sugar's smile temporarily faded as she saw Madison schmoozing with people Sugar didn't know. By the way they were dressed, she guessed they were not from the small hotel but from The Lodge.

The rec room already had many pieces of furniture and chairs, but more seating was brought in. The foosball and Ping-Pong tables were moved to the far wall and converted to dessert tables topped with holiday table-cloths, filled to the brim with Sugar's desserts from the previous shows.

A huge screen covered the windows, blocking the mountain view, and Sugar internally groaned. Seeing herself on a large movie-sized screen was not something she anticipated. As she was embraced in a big bear hug by Paul Anderson, she looked around the room for Jackson.

He was in the back corner of the room, intently listening to a group of snow bunnies who were probably staying at the hotel. One of them touched his arm, and a foreign feeling formed in the pit of her stomach as she fought the urge to go rip the woman's hand off him. He looked up and gave her a wink as she was bombarded by more residents from the town.

Alec dimmed the lights, and everyone took a seat as the show was about to start. Sandwiched between her mom and Eric on one of the comfy couches, Jackson was nowhere in sight. Violet snuggled up to her on her lap, and the room again broke into applause as the show started.

As Tyler the host started announcing the four finalists, Sugar's mind drifted back to that day. So much had changed since then, and it was only a little over six weeks ago.

Sugar sat in her makeup chair and rolled her eyes at her new friend Brittany. "Seriously?" she asked as Brittany donned a pair of antlers that lit up.

"Just giving them what they want," Brittany said as she hit the switch and the lights started dancing. She put a finger to her head and mock shot herself as Sugar shook her head.

There were just four of them left. Sugar, Brittany, Joan, who was a very competitive woman who refused to speak to any other competitors off camera, and Bob the asshole. Thankfully his makeup was already done when they hit the chairs.

They would face off in two rounds before the winner was declared. The first round had an extra hour added to it, and the third round had four hours, up from the normal three. A gift box of Christmas cookies was the first challenge, and the last challenge was a cake. The competitors knew it couldn't be just any cake, but the cake of their life considering the winner would walk away with fifty thousand dollars.

Sugar adjusted her sugarjones.com T-shirt. This week it was the same ice blue color as her eyes and covered in snowflakes. While Brittany ramped up her holiday cheer, Sugar kept to her normal uniform she wore the entire show—yoga pants and some form of sugarjones.com shirt. The only new addition today was a pair of dangly snowflake earrings she boosted from Becca that morning.

The production assistant corralled them to set. Tension was high among staff members during the entire production. Normally the show was shot in the spring, not the fall. Bettie Hogan, the show's matriarch, had suffered a health scare late last winter. She couldn't shoot in the spring, and they decided to take the chance shooting kamikaze style rather than do the show without her.

This was all good and well with Sugar. It made for long days, but she was away from her daughter far less this way. Instead of being spread out over a month, they were attempting to do the show in two weeks, editing teams and producers working round the clock so the show would be ready.

The days were even longer because they recorded the confessionals as soon as the episode was done. Most days started at two or three a.m. and ended well past six. All the contestants were tired. Everybody was tired.

In full-on hyper focus mode, Sugar began calculating what it would take to do the cookies and treats she wanted to do. They needed to make at least three different cookies and could fill the big ornate box on their station with other treats.

Decorated cookies needed to be the star of the first round. In her opinion, it was her best recipe. Almost shortbread- like, the recipe was very simple but incredibly delicious. Sugar knew simple done right was perfection. The amount of time to do them right was a problem, but her brain mentally ticked off the ways she'd accomplish it.

They also sold out almost immediately when she put them on the cookie app back home, and this would raise demand if the judges liked them. Wanting to start a bakery once Violet was in school full-time, leveling up the business was mandatory.

"Good luck," Brittany said sincerely. The lighting and sound people were leaving the set, and the show was about ready to start.

Sugar smiled. "You too, girl," she said. She turned toward the sound of a snort.

"They'll keep that ass of yours on the show until the bitter end," Bob sneered. "You don't need luck."

Bob made comments like this to her the entire time. Insecurity was the root of his problem—Sugar was sure he didn't want to be beaten by a "girl." Refusing to let him get to her, Sugar simply flipped him off.

"Classy."

The executive producer, a young woman with a Napoleon complex, clapped her hands. "We are almost ready." The poor woman seemed stressed beyond measure and was not very pleasant the entire shoot. She kicked a wayward ornament out of the way and stormed off the set, her high heels clicking away.

All the extra baking tables were removed from the set, with the four competitors facing each other in a square. Red, green, and gold decorations weaved throughout the set, and a lowly production assistant scampered after the ornament and placed it back on the big tree.

"Why are you doing it like that?" Tyler Smith asked as Sugar rolled out her dough between two sheets of waxed paper. The bakers were all in full beast mode, getting their doughs ready and watching the clock.

"When you roll dough in flour, it can make it tough. Doing it this way ensures a tender cookie and it doesn't need rolled again when you go to cut it out," Sugar said as she moved one sheet to the side and began work on a second. "The surface size is smaller too, so it chills faster."

She heard Bob snort next to her. Bob was also doing a sugar cookie but put a big lump of dough in the refrigerator already. Sugar worried for a second knowing Bob flavored his cookies with different spices instead of going the simple, classic route. She shook off the nerves knowing Bob was not good at decorating, and hers would be delicious and beautiful.

"You don't agree, Bob?" Tyler said with a fake smile plastered on his face. Sugar was pretty sure every person involved in the show was tired of Bob.

"If you know what you're doing and your recipe is right, you don't need elementary school tricks," he said.

For the millionth time, Sugar wondered how this man got on the show. Did he portray himself differently during the interview process? This show was usually very happy-feely and full of cheer, with contestants helping each other, not knocking each other down.

You couldn't get a more stereotypical, toxic, chauvinistic male chef if you tried.

"*Actually, a wonderful woman with twelve grandchildren taught me to do that,*" *Sugar said.* "*Nobody bakes like Grandma.*" *Picking up her sheets, she jogged to the refrigerator.*

"*What is his deal?*" *Brittany whispered to Sugar as they both reached the refrigerator at the same time. Tyler was now talking to Joan, and all the cameras were focused on the duo.*

"*I was just wondering how the hell he even got on this show,*" *Sugar said. She placed her sheets of dough in the refrigerator and helped Brittany when she noticed she was precariously balancing two cookie sheets of truffles.*

"*It's almost like this is on purpose,*" *Brittany pondered.* "*Bob getting picked to begin with—how Hunter acts toward you. I wonder if they are going for a different narrative this year?*"

Sugar shrugged her shoulders and shut the door to the refrigerator. "*Maybe,*" *she said and ran back to her workstation. It was time to start the chocolate chip cookies.*

Once all the treats were finished, the judges dealt out their critiques and compliments. Bob got the usual compliment that his desserts were delicious but lacked on design. Brittany had the opposite—hers were bang on in the design department but could use a punch of flavor. Poor Joan didn't even finish, pretty much guaranteeing she wouldn't be moving on to the final round.

Sugar took a deep breath as they approached her baking station. Her decorative box turned out exactly how she planned it in her head. Rows of ornament macaroons, chocolate chip cookies, English toffee, coffee fudge, and her delicately decorated sugar cookie snowflakes lined up like proud soldiers. Pretzels decorated with white chocolate and sprinkles defined the clean rows.

The judges tried each of the treats as Sugar held her breath. "*I was skeptical when you described a simple sugar cookie,*" *Hunter* said. "It is exquisite. From the crumb to the flavor, it is absolute perfection. This might be the best cookie I've ever eaten."

Sugar, not one to blush, did so. "Thank you," she said. All her life Sugar fought to be taken seriously, and it was genuinely moving to receive praise like this.

Sugar heard the executive director clear her voice off set and Hunter continued. "These are exquisite. Almost as exquisite as you," he said with a wink. Sugar just shook her head and rolled her eyes as Bettie stepped in to admonish him and give her own thoughts on the cookie.

Everyone in the room started applauding as the judges began tasting Sugar's gift box, bringing her out of her thoughts. She gave Violet a little hug when she saw she was sitting there, fingers crossed, watching the show.

Her mouth dropped wide open as the people gathered in the room started booing. "That's not how it happened," Sugar said in protest but was shushed by the room as Bettie began heaping praise on Sugar.

They had taken out all the compliments Hunter said and only showed the creep factor one. To top it off, they replaced Sugar's response with the one from his original comment, making it seem like Sugar was uncomfortable and embarrassed by his remarks.

She looked to Emery who was sitting on the other side of Becca. She shrugged her shoulders, just as bewildered as Sugar. The two of them had painstakingly gone over every minute of the show while Sugar was shooting, so Emery knew this wasn't right either.

The screen cut to Sugar's confessional. She felt a little uneasy at this part. The day seemed like it stretched out forever, and Sugar was completely exhausted.

Remembering that she got a little emotional, she just hoped it wasn't too emotional.

"The sugar cookies were my husband, Josh's, favorite cookies. He's been gone for five years now. None of this," Sugar said, *gesturing around the small confessional booth, "would have happened without him."*

Off screen the producer leaned forward. "I know it's hard losing your husband, but he was also your business partner. Have you replaced Josh with another partner at Sugar Jones LLC?"

"No!" Sugar exclaimed, and remembering she was to state everything in a sentence instead of like she was answering a question, she added, "No one could ever replace Josh. He's irreplaceable. Josh was funny, smart, innovative . . . He was just everything."

Tears welled up in Sugar's eyes and she blinked rapidly. "I can't talk about this," she said so quietly you could barely hear it, and it had to be closed captioned on the screen.

"Are you okay, Mommy," Violet asked, her little voice quivering.

Sugar's heart almost exploded looking into her little girl's worried eyes. "Mommy's just fine," she said as she felt Eric's arm go around her as her mom squeezed her arm.

She gave Eric and Becca a reassuring smile and engulfed her daughter in a hug. Sugar was so tied up with Violet that she missed the out of context line. The producer's comments weren't shown on screen, so to the rest of the world, it sounded like Sugar would never love anyone but Josh.

Thankfully the show sprung back to action and Joan was eliminated, leaving Sugar, Bob, and Brittany. Sugar remembered her adrenaline being at an all-time high with so much at stake. During the competition she proved she could bake, which was her purpose for being there, but then all she could think about was winning.

Sugar looked over at Brittany frantically making what looked to be snowball cookies, seemingly to be a decoration on her cake. "Just take a deep breath," she thought, willing her friend not to lose it now. Brittany and her husband had a small, struggling bakery and this show meant so much for them.

Sugar's cakes were the first out of the oven and cooling in the blast freezer. A rich, dense deep chocolate intensified by coffee, it was one of her favorite cakes. Strong enough for carving but with a pleasant texture, it was perfect for building her Christmas tree.

Sugar ran to the oven to retrieve her roasted white chocolate. By roasting it, the chocolate wasn't so sickeningly sweet and would give a texture element to her cake. It would be mixed in her peppermint ganache that was setting up in the refrigerator.

Panic almost set in when she stepped up to the oven. Something had a burnt smell, and thankfully it wasn't her chocolate. Taking it out of the oven she called to Bob, "Hey, you better check your cakes."

Rushing back to her station with the hot pan, Bob just shook his head. "Whatever, blondie. I've made this cake a million times. You're not going to rattle me."

"Whatever. I hope the judges like burnt cake," Sugar said as she slid the pan into the shelf to let it cool and began turning the little round sugar cookies into ornaments with royal icing.

She could tell Bob was trying to act all cool, and he finished molding his fondant garland before casually strolling over to the oven. Sugar heard him curse under his breath as he pulled the cakes out. Yep, they were really burnt now. There was no coming back from a burnt cake. Even if you cut it off, the taste permeated the entire cake.

He would need to start over, and Sugar was amazed when he simply threw them in the blast freezer. His pride wouldn't allow him to admit she was right, and it was going to cost him fifty thousand dollars.

Thankfully everything went almost to plan, and Sugar was putting the final touches on her cake. She used zero fondant, using a spatula and piping the branches with buttercream. She was glad she chilled her frosting longer than normal, because the hot studio lights were doing her no favors. Her hand was killing her from pushing the almost solid frosting through the bag, but it would be perfect by judging.

Brittany was not so lucky. Sugar's heart went out to her as she saw her North Pole cake was literally melting. Over the years Sugar watched countless baking competition shows, but she never realized all the pitfalls and problems these bakers faced. Silently she apologized to all the bakers she had called an idiot over the years.

Out of the corner of her eye, she saw Bob icing his cake precariously close to the edge of his station. "Why on Earth would he do that?" Sugar thought as she placed the last decoration on her cake. It was perfect.

It was then she noticed his other hand gently inching the cake to the edge of the table. He was going to drop it on purpose. Just as it was about to tumble, Sugar sprang into action, catching it before it fell to the floor.

Bob looked at her with pure fury. "Thanks," he said between gritted teeth. The buzzer signaled time was up and Sugar sweetly smiled at him. "No problem whatsoever!"

The contestants lined up in front of the judges, ready for their final panel. As Sugar suspected, Bob was dinged not only for *lack of decoration on his monochromatic white cake he deemed "modern," but also on taste.*

They loved Brittany's gingerbread cake, and her version of Santa's workshop was cute as a button, but not quite finished. The icing was melting off the cake as she was being judged, and Sugar's heart went out to her new friend. Sure, Sugar wanted to win, but she didn't want her friend to fail.

"That was quite a catch," judge Harry said, speaking of Sugar saving Bob's cake. "Most wouldn't be so helpful in a contest worth fifty thousand dollars."

"Make no mistake," Sugar said as she crossed her arms across her chest. "While it's true I try to be helpful, that had nothing to do with being helpful and all to do with him having no other excuse except I'm better than him."

Sugar came out of her thoughts as the crowd in the rec room broke into cheers and the screen showed Sugar in the confessional tilting her head and saying, "Boom."

Once declared the winner on the show, Alec brought out a replica of the cake she'd made. The chocolate and peppermint cake with roasted white chocolate and seven-minute fluffy icing for snow was a smashing success. Decorated with cookies, truffles, and topped with a delicate gold star made of sugar, it was simply stunning.

Smiling and thanking another random well-wisher, Sugar looked around the room for Jackson again. A pit began to form in her stomach thinking he might have left with those girls. It would be his right—she was the one that avoided all talk about any kind of commitment from him.

Maybe it was the crowd. Jackson didn't like noisy, and

he didn't like crowded. Her feelings were a little hurt that he didn't watch the show. Perhaps it's for the best. Being just good friends might be a better plan.

CR

"Hey boy," Jackson said to Thor as he entered the man cave. Throwing his keys on the table, he opened the refrigerator and took a beer out. Plopping down in the comfortable recliner, he was surprised when Thor jumped up with him.

Chuckling, he petted Thor's head as he snuggled into his side. Not one to be left out, Poppy jumped up in his lap.

"You always know when I need you, don't you boy?" he said as Thor looked up at him with adoring eyes, tail thumping on the armrest of the chair.

This situation was all his fault. Trapped by a few guests at the beginning of Sugar's party, he couldn't get to her before it began. God, she was so damn good on that show, until he felt like he'd been punched in the gut with her confession about Josh.

Jackson wasn't naive enough to believe that he would be Sugar's first love, even if she was his. He could admit that now—he loved her. A widow with a child, she obviously loved someone deeply in the past, and he was fine with it.

Sugar never talked about her husband, and anytime Jackson tried to bring up a discussion about the two of them, she deflected to something else. He chalked it up to all the changes she faced over the last couple of months. All the new relatives, new move, and new business was enough to make anyone lose their mind.

Now it was clear. Sugar never intended to be with anyone else, and being such a good person, she didn't want to hurt his feelings. Violet's school was out for Christmas vacation since it was only a few days away. Maybe he could get his hurting heart under control by the time she went back.

He'd have to learn to be just friends with Sugar, but one thing was for certain—he wouldn't stop caring about either one of them.

Chapter 12

WIND RATTLED THE WINDOWS like an angry giant was shaking the whole café and apartment upstairs. Peering through them, Sugar could see nothing but snow, snow, and more snow. A storm was hitting Snow Valley and hitting it hard. It was only supposed to last until nighttime but would do enough damage.

The damage would come in the form of a very disappointed little girl on Christmas morning. Sugar felt like kicking one of the giant Santa ornaments across the room. The one time in her life when she was actually ahead of schedule with Christmas presents and Violet wasn't going to get the one thing she wanted more than anything else.

It was supposed to arrive on the twenty-second. Sugar didn't start panicking until it was delayed again on the twenty-third, and according to her tracking app, it was just one town away now. There was no way any deliveries were going to be made in this mess. Yes, people in these mountain towns were used to bad weather, but you couldn't see a hand in front of your face out there.

Thankfully Violet was engrossed with Rudolph on

television and didn't notice her foul mood. Everyone was back at The Lodge, and Becca tried to talk Sugar into coming there before the storm hit. Still holding out hope that a miracle would bring Violet's present, she stubbornly refused. Besides, she kept her employees home and sold all the pre-orders they made herself. They were mostly for people who lived around the square like Sugar; no one else would be coming out today.

The timer went off and Sugar headed to the kitchen to check on dinner. The smell of roast beef filled the air as she opened the oven and slid the homemade rolls inside.

She thought about Jackson and shut the door with more force than was necessary. The night of the finale she finally broke down and texted him, asking where he went. He just answered back he had to take care of a problem with The Lodge, but he was proud of her.

It just didn't fit. That was the last communication they traded. While she knew they weren't in a committed relationship, she felt things were headed that way. With Violet on break, he didn't have an excuse to come over every morning anymore. Perhaps that's why he was always around—to make sure Violet was safe.

"Mom, when this is over, can I watch *Trolls*?" Violet asked from the living room.

If she never heard the word *Trolls* again it would be too soon. Damn snowstorm. "We'll see. It's getting close to dinner time."

Violet got up and looked out the window. "We'll be able to go to Grandma and Grandpa's tomorrow, right?"

Sugar went over to Violet and stood next to her, watching the swirling snow. "Don't you worry about that. Grandpa has all kinds of snowmobiles and said he'd come get us if he had to." Seeing an in, she added, "But tonight is going to be bad out there. Even Santa might have trouble."

Violet giggled and raced back to the couch. "Don't be silly, Mommy! He has a sleigh and Rudolph! His nose shines bright so he can see," said as she clasped her hands together. "I can't wait to get my Troll Lego set! I've been a good girl, right?"

Damn Rudolph to hell, thought Sugar.

"You have been the best girl ever," Sugar said as she felt her soul start to die a slow, miserable death. Then and there she decided to donate triple to Toys for Tots next year. How did parents handle this when they simply couldn't afford to get their child what they wanted?

Sugar followed Becca's lead and had one present from Santa each year. Of course Violet got other things from Sugar, Becca, Emery, and her parents, but just one came from Santa. She'd just have to pick one of the other presents to give to her from Santa.

When Sugar's phone began singing "White Christmas," it almost pushed her over the edge. The temptation to smash it to bits stopped when she saw it was Becca. Her mom never called as she preferred to video chat.

"Hey, what's up, Mom?" Sugar asked as she answered.

"Am I on speaker?" Becca asked.

"No," Sugar said, her curiosity piqued. A phone call and secrecy—two things not in Becca's wheelhouse.

"Listen, your dad went to get Violet's present. It might be late when he gets there, so don't be scared when someone comes in from the café. I don't know how long it'll take."

Sugar's mouth dropped open. "Why would he do

that?" she asked as she went into her bedroom and closed the door partway. "It's dangerous!" Sugar wanted Violet to have the present she wanted, but not at the cost of a life.

"Your dad has been part of search and rescue since he was a teenager, and visibility has improved. He'll be fine and wouldn't go if he couldn't do it. Jackson went with him as backup," her mother added.

Sugar started pacing in her bedroom. "The post office isn't going to be open."

"Oh Sugar, when are you going to realize that people do what your father wants?" Becca sighed. "It might not be right, but it's the truth. If he had to go out at four a.m., he was going to make sure Violet had that present, so he had a carrier he knows take it home with them."

"I don't know what to say," Sugar said, completely dumbfounded.

"Say thank you for starters," Becca said with a laugh. "I have to go now, things are insane around here. Half The Lodge lost power and some of the cabins in the back. Alec and Paul are out there doing what they can and I'm helping Vonnie keep the guests calm."

After hanging up, Sugar walked to the big storybook windows in her apartment. The wind was still whipping away, but not as bad. She could make out the tall light poles around the square with their twinkling lights. She hugged herself and tried not to worry as she looked out at the storm.

CR

Jesus Christ, it was cold. The man was having a hard time feeling his feet as he blindly tried to find the Snow Globe

Café. Sugar was not going to get away with ignoring him. How dare she!

Was it that much to ask for a little communication? He'd been emailing her for weeks now and nothing, not even an acknowledgment of his existence. It ate and ate at him until he couldn't take it anymore. Hopping on a plane, he was here in no time.

This internet age made it easy to find her. She never said she lived above this café, but yep, there she was, standing in the window. A few calls to businesses around town revealed that little fact. His hands were starting to go numb and he began to wonder if this was a good idea. He did fine in his rented SUV until a few blocks from here. He was lucky the storm let up just a little as he started to walk.

Finding an alley next to the café, he followed it until he reached the back and saw a staircase leading upstairs. He figured that must go to the apartment.

He climbed the stairs, his feet painfully prickling with every step. His hands were starting to freeze up, and by the time he got to the door at the top, he just wanted in.

Trying to pound on the door was pointless. With the wind revving up again, he doubted she'd hear it. *I'm going to die out here*, he thought. No, he wasn't going to die, not for a woman who didn't have the common decency to answer him.

Backing away as far as he could, he used all the strength he had left and rammed the door with his shoulder, breaking it free.

Stumbling in the door he saw Sugar grab her daughter and put her behind her. An alarm was ringing through the apartment, and he jerked off his facemask.

"What are you doing here?" Sugar asked.

Violet clamped her hands over her ears and looked up at her mother with frightened eyes. "It's okay, monkey," Sugar said as she ran to the keypad and typed a few numbers in. Shit. She raced back and grabbed her phone to look up the security code.

"You better have a damn good reason for breaking my door down," Sugar said. "Hunter, what are you doing here?"

Hunter Solomon was busy trying to get the door to shut at all. The lock splintered the door clean through. He finally got it to shut and shook his hands.

"Trying not to freeze to death," he said.

"Well come on in," Sugar said with concern as she realized just how cold he was. He didn't have on proper boots or gloves to be out in this weather, and he was incredibly pale.

"You shouldn't sit over here," Violet told him, taking him by the hand and leading him away from the fireplace. "Sit on the couch 'cuz if you have frostbite, you need to warm up slowly," she explained.

Hunter sat down on the couch and took off his boots. "Mommy, we need a pan with warm water," Violet said.

"Yes, we're fine," Sugar said. "I'll send a text to let everyone else know." Becca had called when she received the alert that there was a security breach at the apartment. Sugar could not get the code to work, so she just knocked the alarm off the wall.

"Thank you, baby Jesus," she said as the house went quiet. "Now what, Violet?"

"Umm, we need to put his feet and hands in warm water. Grandpa taught me," she said proudly.

After assuring the police she was fine when they called, Sugar sent off a quick group text to everyone so they wouldn't worry. She filled a bucket and large mixing bowl with lukewarm water and brought it to Hunter. He gingerly put his feet in it, wincing as he slowly lowered them in.

Sugar headed toward the linen closet and got out her mom's old comforter. Hunter took his coat off and wrapped it around himself. "Thank you," he said as he took the bowl of water from Sugar, slowly lowering his hands into the warm water.

"You have to do this for fifteen years," Violet said seriously.

"Wow, I'm going to be here a while, huh?" Hunter said with a grin. "What would you like for your high school graduation?"

When he first burst in the door, it terrified Sugar. Who would have thought that door could be broken so easily? Once she realized who it was, the terror subsided, but the look of him was scary enough. Hunter looked pale and exhausted, a far cry from his rugged handsome self.

He looked much better now. His color was returning and his dark eyes more lifelike. Hunter was a good-looking guy. If Sugar had to guess, he was of Italian descent, with dark hair and olive skin. Standing next to each other, they saw eye to eye, so he probably measured five foot ten.

After checking Google on her phone, Sugar said, "Not quite that long. Ten, fifteen minutes, you should be good to go."

"You're not going to throw me back outside, are you?" Hunter asked skeptically. "I'm really sorry I broke your door and scared you and your little girl. I thought for sure I was a goner out there."

The timer went off for dinner, and Sugar headed to the kitchen to take it out. "Don't tempt me. I can't even imagine the mathematical chances that you just happened upon my apartment in the middle of a storm they've been predicting for three days."

Tenting the meat so it could rest, Sugar then put the homemade rolls on a rack to cool. "I suppose you want me to feed you too."

"That'd be great," he said, turning his head toward the kitchen. "It smells delicious."

"Fine, but if you tell me to smile, I'm throwing you back out into the cold," Sugar said as she came and sat in her favorite chair with her favorite quilt.

Water splashed in the bowl and threatened to come spilling out as he turned to face Sugar. "Yeah, about that. That's kind of why I'm here. I figured you knew what went on once the show aired. They air a character, not a person. They decided to hate my character this season."

Sugar snorted. "You couldn't be portrayed that way if you didn't say those things," she said as Violet crawled into her lap.

Hunter's brow wrinkled. "Is that why you wouldn't answer me?"

"Answer you?" Sugar asked. "I haven't heard anything from you."

Hunter shook his head. "No, I've emailed and called, and a lady named Vanessa would not put me through to you."

It was all starting to make sense now. Hunter was part of the show, so Vanessa, ever the pitbull, blocked him, and following Sugar's orders, would wait until after the holidays before passing on any show communication. Sugar explained this to Hunter, who nodded in understanding.

"I've had so much going on. I didn't have this café when we filmed the show. I only had a short period to get it ready before we aired, so I couldn't deal with any of that," Sugar explained.

"I think I'm good here," Hunter said, pulling his hands out of the water.

"Monkey, can you go get Mr. Hunter a towel?" Sugar asked.

"Yep! Be right back!" she said, always happy to be helping.

As she was coming back from the bathroom, the apartment door crashed open. Again.

A bat wielding Madison rushed into the apartment. In a jet-black snow suit and black hat, she looked like an adorable cat burglar. "Get away from them before I bash your head in," she warned.

"Whoa, whoa, Madison," Sugar said as she stood up. "What are you doing?"

Madison's arm holding the bat went limp as she took in the room. "I . . . I thought you and Violet were in trouble. The alarm has been going off for almost an hour. My dad and Jackson are gone, Alec and Paul are at the back cabins, and I didn't wait to find your mom."

Violet threw the towel at Hunter and rushed to embrace her aunt. "Hi Aunt Madison! I haven't seen you in forever!"

Madison dropped the bat and hugged her little niece.

"I'm afraid that's my fault. I said something not true the last time I was here and hurt your feelings. I'm sorry for that and I was wrong."

"It's okay!" Violet said.

Children were so easy to forgive. In her heart, Sugar knew Madison never meant to hurt Violet and truly cared for her. Anyone who would go out in this storm to protect her daughter, not knowing what they would find at the other end, might just deserve a second chance.

Hunter was busy drying his hands and feet, and Sugar walked over to her sister. "You're an asshole," she said as she embraced her sister.

"I know, but I'll try to do better," Madison said as she embraced her sister back, her relief on finding them alright breaking through her stone walls.

Madison joined the trio, and with her expertise added to Violet's limited knowledge on people exposed to the cold. She recommended Hunter take a warm bath. Sugar gathered his clothes to dry after he hilariously put on one of Sugar's psychedelic robes and headed to the old-fashioned claw foot tub in the bathroom.

"What's he doing here?" Madison asked as Sugar got dinner ready to serve.

Sugar was carving the roast into pieces and looked up. "Not sure. I was about to find out when a bat wielding lunatic showed up."

Madison slightly blushed. "You really should tell people when there isn't a problem."

Sugar strained the vegetables and put them in their own dish. "I did. I sent out a group text, but I don't have your phone number."

She lived here for nearly two months and didn't have

her own sister's phone number. Granted, Madison was never the most welcoming, but considering she was Violet's aunt, maybe she should have taken the initiative to get to know her—even a little.

Trusting her would never be easy. She dealt with too many girls with the same qualities as Madison to be that stupid. Sugar also knew some of those girls changed when they got older and out of the cesspool that was high school. Most were merely trying to survive those adolescent years without being scarred too badly.

Every time she ran into one of those people from high school, either ones who spread rumors or simply did nothing to stop them, she was always surprised that every one of them acted like they were old friends. Most didn't even realize the carnage they caused. Kids were just trying to survive the drama that was high school and get out as unscathed as possible. Wrapped up in their own problems, teenagers are usually to shortsighted to see the problems of others.

That didn't mean she needed to alienate her either. Sugar would just need to take it one baby step at a time. One thing was certain—if she ever did something to hurt Violet again, intentional or not, it was over.

"I suppose that would be my fault," Madison said. "I haven't been exactly welcoming. I'm not good with new people under ordinary circumstances, unless they are guests."

After placing the meat and vegetables on a very cool 1950s Christmas serving dish she found in the back of the pantry, she filled a wicker basket with the homemade rolls. Maybe she and Madison weren't so different after all and used separate paths to deal with their trust issues.

"Same," said Sugar. She brought dinner to the table. "I guess for our parents' sake we should try to get along."

That was another thing they had in common. Madison loved her dad just as much as Sugar loved her mom.

"Yes, you are right," Madison said, "but if you use that word 'same' again, I'm afraid I simply can't be related to you."

Sugar smiled and flipped her off. "Violet, come eat dinner," she called.

Hunter stepped out of the bathroom in the colorful robe looking just as foolish as before. "Did someone say dinner?" he asked with his charming smile.

Soon bellies were full, and plates were cleared. Small talk around the table was a bit awkward, which soon turned into full blown awkward for Sugar when she realized Hunter seemed to have a thing for Madison. Sugar didn't bring up why the hell Hunter unceremoniously showed up at her door, guessing it might not be for Violet's ears.

"Mom, I need to talk to you," Violet whispered loudly as they all settled into the living room.

Sugar took Violet's outstretched hand and let her lead her into the bedroom.

"Can I make Mr. Hunter a present? He's stuck here and won't have a Christmas present," Violet said with big, worried eyes.

Kneeling, Sugar engulfed her little girl in a bear hug. "That is about the kindest thing I've ever heard, Violet, and it makes Mommy very proud of you."

She felt a catch in her throat as she hugged her daughter tighter, so very grateful for this little girl. Maybe the universe knew it threw enough at her during her short life, so it gave Sugar this sweet child.

Sugar retrieved her craft supplies from the top of the closet, and Violet went to town. She already made bedazzled pet rocks for every person she knew in Snow Valley, and now Hunter would get his very own. Closing the door partway, Sugar headed for her favorite chair.

Hunter and Madison were sitting on the couch, engrossed in a conversation about wine. Sugar cleared her throat. "So, what the fuck, Hunter?" she said, forgetting her vow to curb her use of profanity. Violet was in the other room anyway.

"Yes, well I suppose you wonder why I'm here," he said as he played with the belt ends of Sugar's robe. "As I said before, you wouldn't answer my calls and I became a bit desperate."

"How so?" Sugar asked as she picked up her cup of cocoa. She thought she may need something stronger in this by the time the night was over.

Hunter smiled sheepishly. "Well, I guess I was hoping you'd come to bat for me, and that seems to run in the family," he said as he grinned and winked at Madison.

"Hunter, I have no idea what you are talking about," Sugar said in obvious confusion.

Looking rather uncomfortable, he cleared his throat. "Look, the show portrayed me in a way that isn't fair. I know I didn't have to say the things they led me to say, but that's how it goes in the business. I guess I was hoping you'd, I don't know, defend me?" he asked lamely.

Ah, so this is why he was here. Emery had mentioned she wondered how the negative press would affect him. Sugar was so busy since the show aired, she didn't have time to think about it, and she rarely got on social media for anything other than business.

"Defend you how?" Sugar asked as she raised an eyebrow.

Hunter threw his arms up in the air. "Do you have any idea how hard it was for me to come here? They are eating me alive on social media. Two of my restaurants have women head chefs. Two. Those women aren't going to have a job for long if this continues and my doors close."

"What have you done about it?" Madison asked. "Have you denied you're the sexist pig they portray you as, or do you just want Sugar to come out and say it?"

Hunter leaned back into the couch. "It wouldn't do any good. Everything I worked for—everything—is about to be done for over some woman. My investors are this close to backing out," he said, pinching his fingers together.

"And now I'm some woman?" Sugar laughed and tucked her long legs underneath herself. "That's not exactly the way to get me to help you."

Hunter sighed. "Not you. That came out wrong. Jamie."

Sugar's brows came together. Jamie was the producer with a Napoleon complex on the show. Sure, she was way uptight, but everyone was stressing on set.

"We kind of had a thing, and then we didn't. The show never would have let it go down like that, but because of how we had to shoot it once the 'Let's kill Hunter' train was rolling, there was no stopping it," Hunter explained.

Sugar got up, needing to move. She walked to the front windows and looked out. At least you could see relatively clearly now. Snatching Branch out of the tree, she started to pace in front of Hunter and Madison. "So what am I supposed to do?"

Hunter sighed. "Look, I can't say anything bad about the show. My career would be over."

"But it's okay for Sugar to kill her career?" Madison asked, narrowing her eyes at Hunter.

"It would be different for her, and you know it," Hunter said. "Besides, she never fell for their balderdash when they tried to get her to play a role. Everyone else played the game, but not her."

Sugar let a struggling Branch down and was relieved he decided to haughtily stalk into Violet's room instead of climbing the tree again.

"We aren't going to figure this out tonight. It's Christmas Eve," she said looking out the window again.

Madison stood and joined her sister at the window. "They're going to be fine," she said, correctly guessing that Sugar was still worried about Eric and Jackson. "They've been in worse weather than this. It's part of living where we live, especially if you're on the emergency response team."

The dryer buzzed in the small laundry room in the kitchen. "I got it," Hunter said, obviously grateful to get out of Sugar's silly robe.

"Listen," Madison said, lowering her voice as Hunter went into the bathroom to change. "I'm really sorry if I caused problems between you and Jackson. None of you have confronted me about it, but I correctly guessed Violet knew what I said by the way he was acting. He deserves to be happy."

Sugar sighed. "There is no Jackson and me. He really was just being nice for Violet's sake." She intently peered out the window. "I haven't seen him since the finale aired, and I barely saw him that night."

Madison gently touched Sugar's shoulder to gain her attention. "I've known Jackson my whole life, and he is crazy about you. He wouldn't have gotten so close to Violet if he weren't. Maybe he felt insecure about it all after what you said about Violet's dad on the show."

Sugar turned to face Madison. "What did I say about Josh?" she said with a quizzical expression. She remembered getting emotional about replacing him at Sugar Jones LLC, but that was it.

"How you could never replace him?" Madison said. "It sounded like you'd never even look at another man again."

She thought back to the finale but didn't really hear that part because Violet got worried about seeing her mom upset. They must have edited it to look like something completely different.

"I was talking about the business. They asked me about who took his spot in the business," Sugar said.

Madison turned back to the window and peered into the darkness. "You should talk to him. He sees good in everything, even me," she said in a small voice. "Well, he used to. I believe gossiping in front of Violet may have taken me off that list for good."

"I don't trust people easily," Sugar said.

"Same," Madison said as they both looked at each other and smiled.

Sugar put her arm around her sister's shoulder. "I do believe I'm rubbing off on you."

"God help me."

The bathroom door opened, and Hunter stepped out. He looked much more secure in his jeans and navy knitted sweater. "Thank God I'm out of that robe."

A knock came from the kitchen door that led to the bakery, and Eric and Jackson stepped through the door.

Dressed in warm black snow suits with reflective yellow strips down the arms and back, both were in much better shape than Hunter when he arrived.

"Grandpa! Jackson!" Violet said as she ran from her room to greet her two favorite men. Eric scooped her up into a bear hug.

"Hey there, little bug, you all ready for Santa?" he asked.

Violet clasped her little hands together. "Oh yes, I've been a good girl!"

"The very best," he said, kissing her forehead. "I need to talk to your mommy for a minute, okay?"

Sugar hadn't taken her eyes off Jackson the entire time. She saw a sadness reflected back in his eyes, but he gave her a small smile.

Putting Violet back on the ground, he finally noticed the other people in the room. "What's going on here?"

"Long story," Sugar said. "You said you needed to talk to me? We can go into my room."

They went into her room and closed the door. Eric took off his backpack and produced her daughter's one wish—a *Trolls* Lego set. "Ta da!" he said with a smile.

"Why would you do that?" Sugar asked. "You . . . you shouldn't have put yourself at risk! Something horrible could have happened to you!"

Eric placed his precious cargo on her bed. "Sug, it was fine. I would have waited until later if I thought it was too dangerous," he said. Placing a hand on her shoulder, he searched her eyes. "When your mom told me about this, how upset you were, how could I not do it?"

Sugar took a deep breath and slowly let it out, desperately trying to keep her raging emotions in check. "I appreciate it, I really do," she said. "Violet would have been fine. Even if you all are used to this weather, something bad still could have happened."

"I know Violet would have been fine. But what about you? I didn't do this for Violet, sweetheart. I did this for you," Eric said softly. "It's what fathers do."

He was right. Sugar would have kicked herself for years if Violet didn't get this present. She didn't know if Becca filled him in on her habit of blaming herself for things, or if he'd observed it himself. It didn't matter.

"Thank you, Dad," she said as she threw her arms around him, tears flowing from her eyes.

Eric embraced her back, resting his cheek on top of her head. "You're welcome, sweetheart," he said with a hitch in his voice.

The two walked out of the bedroom hand in hand, and found Hunter filling a skeptical Jackson in on why he was there. It was decided that Hunter would spend the night at Emery's since she was back at The Lodge with her parents.

"Mom, it's time for bed!" Violet announced to the room, giving the visitors the eye.

Santa Claus was the best idea ever, and not for the first time, Sugar wished Santa came at least once a month. Not only did Violet eat all her dinner without being reminded once, she now was insisting it was bedtime.

She handed Hunter the keys to the apartment next door, and hugged Eric and Madison. "Be careful," she said.

"Always," Eric responded as he picked up Violet. "Don't worry, little one, we are going so Santa can come."

Violet threw her little arms around her grandpa's neck

and gave him a kiss on the cheek. Jackson was zipping his snowsuit back up, and Madison gave Sugar a little nod in his direction.

Sugar placed her hand on Jackson's, stopping his progress. She looked up into his eyes. "Can you stay for a while?" she asked.

A range of emotions flittered across his face, but he nodded in agreement.

Chapter 13

VIOLET ASKED JACKSON to read her "Twas the Night Before Christmas" and was asleep in record time. Sugar was walking to the living room with two cups of steaming hot chocolate when Jackson came out of her room, closing the door softly.

"She's out like a light," he said as he stuffed his hands in his pockets awkwardly. A soft, instrumental version of "White Christmas" was playing, with the lights from the Christmas tree twinkling in the background. The fire blazed in the fireplace, and Jackson looked pure man in his jeans and tight fitting white thermal shirt. She didn't even mind the fact that he'd put his hair back up in the man bun.

"Come, sit," Sugar said as she put down the two cups of cocoa on the coffee table. She sat on the couch instead of her favorite chair because she wanted to be close to him for this.

"Look, I know it might seem like I've been acting weird," Jackson said as he walked to the couch.

"I love you," Sugar said, surprising herself almost as much as Jackson.

Jackson stopped mid-walk and his mouth dropped open. "What did you say?" he asked.

"I probably shouldn't have led with that," Sugar said, embarrassed. "It's something I do, say impulsive things when emotions are high. If you decide to love me back, you'll have to get used to it."

Jackson sat down next to Sugar and she curled her long legs underneath her and turned to face him.

"I don't think that's a decision you get to make," he said. "I'm a little confused here. I thought . . . after the finale, well, I thought that maybe I've been pushing myself on you and you were just being nice."

"No!" Sugar said. "No, that's not true at all. I need to tell you something. Something only Emery knows."

Jackson let out a breath he didn't realize he was holding and took her hand. "You don't have to."

"I do," Sugar said. "I really do need to tell you. I know you know about some of the issues I had in junior high and high school. I was probably around thirteen when it started. Boys who were my friends now made up stories about me. It made me fair game because I was the alleged slut."

Jackson took her hand in his, giving it a gentle squeeze of encouragement.

"So, trusting boys was definitely not my thing. Any time I tried to do anything resembling a date, or even just hang out and surf or whatever like we did in the past, it always turned into a wrestling match or another story being spread around the school."

Sugar pulled her favorite quilt around herself tightly. "Josh was different. Josh was safe. I'd been best friends with him for a few years before we started dating. At first it was great, and then not so much. He was always worried I'd leave him. I'm sure he felt it. I was growing apart from him the older we got. He did a lot to knock down my self-confidence and used my ADHD issues to make everything seem like it was my fault. It's taken me a long time to realize that."

"The night he died, well, for a long time I thought it was my fault." Sugar's mouth was moving, telling Jackson the story, but her mind went back to that night, that awful night when everything changed forever.

"Very good, Sugar!" Joe, the head baker at Kaufman's Bakery exclaimed as Sugar pulled the challah out of the oven. "You need to eat some of that for that little baby. You're still skinny as a rail!"

"I don't feel skinny as a rail," Sugar said. "More like a beached whale." Her hands went instinctively to her growing baby. If she felt like this now, how would she feel in four more months?

She began working on the bagel dough, conscious of the fact that her cell phone was buzzing like crazy in her back pocket. Joe had a strict no cell phone policy at work, and she didn't want to check it anyway. More than likely, Josh was drinking. Again.

After it came out that he was the one who made the decision not to use a condom after making comments about Sugar forgetting her pills, things were incredibly strained between them. She was trying to make this work for their child's sake, but after all of this, his drinking escalated.

At first when the bakery's main line started ringing, Sugar thought nothing of it, but when someone kept calling over and over, a pit started forming in her stomach. He wouldn't call her work, would he?

Her suspicions were confirmed when Joe came back from finally answering it with a grave face. "You need to go call your husband," he said quietly. "Don't worry, I'll erase the messages he left."

Completely mortified, Sugar started apologizing profusely. "Please don't apologize, it's not your fault," Joe said kindly. "If you ever need help, you know you can come to me, right?"

Sugar blinked back the tears and nodded, going outside to call Josh. Joe was a kind man, and she couldn't help but notice the look of pity in his eyes. How had her life turned into this? Almost as soon as she married Josh, she felt she'd made a mistake. Because she never had a father in her life, she wanted her child to have one, but not this kind of man.

She had at least twenty text messages from him, and a couple from Emery. Josh couldn't control himself when he was drinking and would call everyone he knew. Emery would change the password on sugarjones.com the minute she realized he was getting smashed, because he would even post there when he was drunk.

Sugar stood under the awning to protect herself from the cold rain. It was unusual to see rain or cold in California, and the night matched Sugar's gloomy mood. Taking a shuttering breath, she called Josh.

"What the fuck, Sug?" Josh said as he answered the phone. "I needed to talk to you and got some lecture from that jerk you work with. This is bullshit." His words were angry and slightly slurred.

"I'm at work, Josh," Sugar said angrily. "How dare you call my job. Do you know how embarrassing this is? Do you?"

"Oh yes, the all-important job that you don't need. Fuck that. I'm your husband. Does that mean anything to you?"

"Of course it does, and I do need this job. I'm learning a lot here. I don't know how many times we have to go through this." Sugar took one hand and rubbed her aching forehead.

Josh laughed bitterly. "Like that education your mama paid for and your year in France wasn't enough?"

"You can always learn, Josh," Sugar said. She was pacing now and angry. Really angry. Back and forth she paced, cold rain splashing her face on each turn.

"When are you going to put me first? Love me the most?" he asked.

"Maybe when you love me more than you love alcohol," she shot back.

Josh snorted. "Is this what's it's going to be like the rest of our lives? You bitching every time I need to blow off some steam."

"No Josh, it's not going to be like this the rest of our lives because I refuse to live like this," Sugar said. "I can't do this anymore, Josh. We'll talk when I get home."

"You can't just say something like that on the phone," Josh said.

"I didn't say anything. We'll talk when I get home."

"Fuck you, Sugar, don't you dare hang up on me," he shouted, and she did just that.

Her eyes filled with tears as her body felt a resolve she hadn't felt in a long time. Things would be difficult, but she needed to do this. She needed to distance herself from him not only for her child, but for her own sanity.

Wiping her eyes, she texted Emery: Sry about 2night. Josh and I are done. Will talk 2morrow.

"I think that's the only reason Emery knows," Sugar said. "I don't know if I would have had the courage to tell her otherwise. I had so much guilt, like maybe he wouldn't have drove that night if I hadn't said what I said over the phone."

Jackson reached out and pulled Sugar to him, gently cradling her and stroking her hair. "It wasn't your fault."

"I know," Sugar said in a small voice into his chest. Pulling back she looked into his eyes. "I know that now, but it's taken a long time to get there. He wasn't always like that. He was sweet and good and kind and so funny. It wasn't until he started in with the drinking that he changed so much, so I'm kind of fucked up."

"Aren't we all?" Jackson said. When Sugar tilted her head quizzically to the side, he continued. "I don't like crowds or loud noises because of my time in the Army. There was a bomb. It took out half my squad. I don't like to talk about it."

"Oh Jackson," she said as she put her arms around him.

Tilting her head back gently with his thumb, he gave her a small smile. "And as far as making a decision to love you, that was made that day back in October when you popped out of that SUV with the most beautiful little girl. I just didn't know it at the time."

He leaned down and softly kissed her lips. "I love you Sugar, and I've loved you from the minute I laid eyes on you. I always said I wouldn't get involved and would live it up until I was at least thirty-five, but you showed up early."

Sugar laughed. "Would you tell my mother that? She'll never believe I was ever early for anything." His smiling lips came back for another kiss, and she breathed in his scent, that wintery, spicy smell she had grown to love so much.

Climbing onto his lap she deepened it, and his arms pulled her close. "Jesus woman, you are going to be the death of me," he said as he tried to control his ragged breath. "I should go. It's late."

"Or you could stay," Sugar said.

He gently cradled her face with his hands, his thumb massaging her cheek. "If I stay, I'm never going to leave," he warned.

"Promise?" she asked with a smile.

"Promise," he said.

Sugar climbed off him and offered him her hand. The walked hand in hand to her bedroom, first stopping to check on a sleeping Violet.

"You sure this is alright?" Jackson asked as they looked in on the sleeping child.

"Positive," Sugar smiled as they went into her bedroom. She always thought it was a blessing that her child slept like the dead, but never more so than now.

∝

"I need the details," Emery said in a hushed whisper. Allison, Eric's ex-wife was helping Becca with her hair and Violet was twirling around in her adorable green Christmas/flower girl dress. Black patent shoes clicking as she spun round and round.

Sugar, Emery, and Madison wore red dresses in matching fabric all in different styles to suit them. Madison's was off the shoulder with tight sleeves. The front of the dress rose to a tea length, while the back remained long.

Emery's dress was strapless and fitted at the waist, spreading out into a full skirt. Sugar's was more of a Grecian style, with thin straps. It loosely followed the lines of her body, and her hair was up in an elaborate braided updo, one that Violet's hair matched.

Sugar looked both ways and leaned in toward Emery

and Madison. "We screwed each other's brains out," she whispered with a wicked grin.

"OMG, Sugar!" Emery said. "You are hopeless!"

"I'm demanding a DNA test. There is no way we are related," Madison sniffed.

Sugar smiled wider at her friend and sister's obvious disgust. That was one way to shut them up. Truth be told, last night was beautiful and unlike anything she had ever experienced. It was sweet and hot at the same time. By the time Jackson was done with her, she could barely remember her name. She didn't want to share that information with anyone but Jackson. God, she was becoming one of those mushy love people.

"All done!" Allison said as Becca turned to face them. She looked positively gorgeous with her blonde hair in gorgeous finger waves and a simple fitted white dress that hit just below the knee. It showed off the figure Becca worked so hard to keep, and she was positively glowing.

Sugar rushed forward and hugged her mom. Violet joined the two, hugging both their legs.

"Grams, you look beautiful," she said.

"You really do, Mom," Sugar said. "I'm so happy for you."

Her mother, her hero, deserved this and so much more. She went through so much all alone, and Sugar was so happy she reconnected with her dad.

Becca gave her daughter a squeeze. "And I'm happy for you."

"Mom, don't start," Sugar protested.

Cupping her daughter's face, Becca laughed. "Oh, dear child, I can't start because I'll never stop," she said with a wink.

CR

Everyone was gathered in the main house in the opulent living room. A fire raged in the big cobblestone fireplace, and a tree that nearly hit the high ceilings twinkled with white lights and glossy red and green ornaments and bows. With the furniture cleared, they had room to make seating for everyone.

Small and intimate, it was just perfect for Becca. Sugar stood by her mother's side with Madison, Emery, and Violet as they exchanged their vows. She caught Jackson's eye from the groom's side and wiggled her eyebrows. She smiled as he bit his lip to keep from laughing.

"I've dreamed of this since I was eight years old," Becca was saying as she held hands with Eric. "I don't need to promise my love to you because it is already yours, forever. Even apart, I never stopped loving you, not even for a second."

Eric smiled. "The kind of man I am is because of you. You make me better person. You showed me a different way to be, and I will spend the rest of my life showing you just how much I love and appreciate you."

CR

Sugar held her hand to her heart as Jackson danced with little Violet on the dance floor. Eric twirled Becca, and Emery danced with Alec. She seemed to be arguing with him as he just laughed.

Madison walked up next to her sister. "I never thanked you for not telling anyone about what happened to Violet," she said.

"No thanks necessary," she smiled at the sight of Jackson's tall figure bent down, holding Violet's hands as she swayed back and forth. "Today would have been way different if I had. I know my mom, and she wouldn't get over it."

"So you did it for them?" Madison said, gesturing to their respective parents.

"At first, yes. But after last night, I'm glad I kept quiet. Rest assured, if it happens again, I won't."

"Noted," Madison said.

Sugar took the time to process what exactly happened last night and really think about it. Madison jumped on a snowmobile, rode it during a snowstorm and barged into the apartment with nothing but a bat, not knowing what she would find, because she thought Sugar and Violet were in trouble. A bad person simply did not do that, and maybe Madison just needed to have more positive influences in her life.

A couple of old friends of the family walked up. "I'm Harriet," an elderly lady with expensive jewelry and tasteful dress said. "I was friends with your grandmother for years. It's a shame she couldn't make it."

"Nice to meet you," Sugar said as she took the lady's fragile hand.

Shame, indeed. Her grandmother didn't come because she was embarrassed about Sugar and Violet. Her parents didn't come out and say it, but Sugar knew. Eric was a horrible liar, and when he told Sugar that a health problem was preventing her from traveling, Sugar knew it was bullshit.

As far as she was concerned, her long-lost grandma could stay gone forever.

"Just look at Alec! He's grown into such a handsome

young man. Your grandfather would be so proud!" she exclaimed as Madison rolled her eyes.

Harriet went on to socialize with others, and Sugar glanced at her sister. "Everyone sure loves Alec," she said. Since she had arrived in Snow Valley, most people would always steer the conversation to him. She could imagine that would get rather annoying if it happened your whole life.

"Oh yes, Alec, the perfect crowned prince of Snow Valley. Let me tell you, he's not as innocent as everyone thinks," she said.

"What do you mean by that?" Sugar asked.

"Nothing. Turning over a new leaf, remember?"

Well now's a fine time to start, Sugar thought. Hunter came up and asked Madison to dance, just as Jackson was coming back from the dance floor. A more up-tempo song was playing, and Violet was jumping around with Alec, having the time of her life.

"Now's our chance," Sugar said as she grabbed Jackson's hand and led him out of the room and down the hallway to the more private family room with the gorgeous view they shared on Thanksgiving.

The duo plopped down on the couch and Sugar snuggled up to Jackson. "Tired?" he asked.

"Exhausted. I didn't get much sleep last night."

Sugar felt that low, sexy rumble of a laugh ripple through his chest. "I wonder why that is?"

Sugar sighed. "It's a mystery."

"Did you get things straight with Hunter?" Jackson asked. They barely saw each other all day with Christmas and a wedding happening at the same time.

"Yeah. Emery's motto is no publicity is bad publicity,

and me defending the current target of the #metoo movement would get me a lot of publicity." Sugar waved her hand. "Emery took care of it, I guess. She posted a photo of Madison, Hunter, and me."

Jackson started running his fingers along her collar bone, and Sugar involuntarily shivered.

"Cold?" Jackson asked.

"Quite the opposite actually," she replied.

"Mom!" called Violet as she raced into the room and did a flying leap onto her mother's lap.

"They want to cut the cake!" Violet said. "We've got to go!"

"Help me up," Sugar said as Violet jumped down. Grabbing Sugar's hands, Violet pulled and pulled but Sugar didn't budge.

"Come on, Moooom," Violet whined as she pulled harder.

Jackson leaned around Sugar. "I got this, kid." With one fell swoop he had Sugar over his shoulder and was carrying Violet with the other arm.

"Put me down right now, Jackson!"

"Don't. Don't put her down," Violet laughed as he trudged his way to the kitchen. "Are you staying the night again, Jackson?"

"Maybe not," Sugar warned as she slapped at Jackson's butt.

"You should just come stay forever. You can bring Thor and Poppy. We can be a big family!" Violet said.

Jackson put his mouth to Violet's ear and whispered something.

Arriving in the kitchen, Jackson gently set Sugar on the ground. "Wow," he said.

Before him was Eric and Becca's wedding cake. It wasn't a normal wedding cake, but an exact replica of the tree house that started everything. The treehouse where Eric and Becca first met. The treehouse where they fell in love and broke apart. The treehouse where Sugar was conceived. It was perfect.

"Do you mind wheeling it out?" Sugar asked.

"Not at all."

As he started out the door, she knelt down to Violet's level. "What did Jackson whisper to you?"

Violet giggled and put her hand to her mouth. "He said I'm working on it."

Me too Violet, me too, thought Sugar.

She heard the guests break into applause and she took her daughter's hand and walked toward the excitement. In Sugar's short life, change hadn't always signaled something good, but this change, with her newfound family, was one of the best things to ever happen to her. The fact that it didn't scare her made her realize how much she had grown, and how much she had overcome.

The future looked bright indeed, especially now that she finally found her home.

Thank You

I'd like to thank and dedicate this book to my parents, Bob and Sue Calton. You always taught me anything was possible with hard work, and to never give up. While you may be gone now, you will never ever be forgotten.

From the Author

If you enjoyed this book, please leave a review on your favorite platform!

Raised in Northwest Indiana, or "The Region" as it's called, Kelly J Calton wrote her first book, "That Darn Dog" for her first-grade young author's contest.

After creating a popular blog called My 30 Point life documenting the trials and tribulations experienced while losing a significant amount of weight, she decided to focus on writing a book.

Please visit http://www.kellyjcalton.com for updates on book three in the Snow Globe Café series!